A Collection of

Fiction and Essays

by Occult Writers on

Supernatural and

Metaphysical

Subjects

By

Manly P. Hall, Aleister Crowley, Algernon Blackwood, Helena P. Blavatsky, Arthur Machen, Franz Hartmann, Lafcadio Hearn, Lord Dunsany, C. W. Leadbeater, William Q. Judge, H. W. Percival and Richard Garnett

ISBN: 978–1–63118–510-6

Esoteric Classics

Other Books in this Series and Related Titles

The Devil in Love by Jacques Cazotte (978–1–63118–499–4)

Confessions of an English Opium–Eater by T De Quincey (978–1–63118–485–7)

Atlantis, the Gods of Antiquity and the Myth of the Dying God (978–1–63118–498–7)

Qabbalistic Teachings and the Tree of Life by M P Hall (978–1–63118–482–6)

Rosicrucian Rules, Secret Signs, Codes and Symbols by various (978–1–63118–488–8)

The Poem of Hashish by A Crowley & C Baudelaire (978-1-63118-484-0)

Fortune–Telling with Dice by Astra Cielo (978–1–63118–466–6)

The Janeites, The Man Who Would Be King and Other Stories of Freemasonry
by Rudyard Kipling (978–1–63118–480–2)

Crystal Vision Through Crystal Gazing by Achad (978–1–63118–455–0)

Rosa Alchemica, The Tables of Law & The Adoration of the Magi
by William Butler Yeats (978–1–63118–421–5)

The Star and the Garter by Aleister Crowley (978-1-63118-406-2)

Thirty–One Hymns to the Star Goddess by Frater Achad (978–1–63118–422–2)

Ghosts in Solid Form by Gambier Bolton (978–1–63118–469–7)

A Collection of Magical Writings, Fiction, Poetry & Essays
By Aleister Crowley (978–63118–424–6)

The Sword of Welleran and Other Stories by Lord Dunsany (978-1-63118-501-4)

Arcane Formulas or Mental Alchemy by W W Atkinson (978–1–63118–459–8)

The Machinery of the Mind by Dion Fortune (978–1–63118–451–2)

The Legend of the Holy Grail and its Connection with Templars and Freemasons
by A E Waite (978-1-63118-462-8)

The Leadbeater Reader: A Selection of Occult Essays (978–1–63118–483–3)

Audio versions are also available on Audible, Amazon and Apple

Other Books in this Series and Related Titles

Paracelsus, the Four Elements and Their Spirits by M P Hall (978-1-63118-400-0)

The Magician's Heavenly Chaos by Thomas Vaughan (978-1-63118-500-7)

Masonic and Rosicrucian History by M P Hall & H Voorhis (978-1-63118-486-4)

Tao Te Ching & Commentary by Lao Tzu & C Johnston (978-1-63118-495-6)

The Influence of Pythagoras on Freemasonry and Other Essays (978-1-63118-404-8)

The Golden Verses of Pythagoras: Five Translations (978-1-63118-479-6)

Magical Essays and Instructions by Florence Farr (978–1–63118–418–5)

History, Analysis and Secret Tradition of the Tarot by Hall &c (978-1-63118-445-1)

The Kabbalah of Masonry & Related Writings by E Levi &c (978-1-63118-453-6)

A Collection of Early Writings on Astral Travel (978-1-63118-477-2)

The Ceremony of Initiation: Analysis & Commentary (978-1-63118-473-4)

The Old Past Master by Carl H Claudy (978-1-63118-464-2)

The Path of Light: A Manual of Maha-Yana Buddhism (978-1-63118-471-0)

The Hymns of Hermes by G. R. S. Mead (978-1-63118-405-5)

Clairvoyance and Psychic Abilities by Leadbeater & Besant (978-1-63118-403-1)

Catholicism, Yoga and Hinduism by Hartmann &c (978-1-63118-478-9)

American Indian Freemasonry by A C Parker (978-1-63118-460-4)

Ancient Mysteries and Secret Societies by M P Hall (978-1-63118-410-9)

*A Collection of Writings Related to Occult, Esoteric, Rosicrucian and Hermetic Literature,
Including Freemasonry, the Kabbalah, the Tarot, Alchemy and Theosophy*
various authors *Volumes 1-4*
(978-1-63118-713-1) (978-1-63118-714-8)
(978-1-63118-715-5) (978-1-63118-716-2)

Audio Versions are also available on Audible, Amazon and Apple

Table of Contents

Introduction

The unifying factor of this collection is, that without exception, every author included here was in some way or another involved with or interested in the occult. In some cases, they were members of an occult organization, such as the *Hermetic Order of the Golden Dawn*, the *Theosophical Society* or similar such groups. Others simply had a strong personal interest in the subject matter or practiced some form of the esoteric sciences in private, their interests having been preserved through diary entries and letters to their peers or documented by the publishing legacy they left behind. Of the writers presented here, those who primarily limited their writing to fiction, almost always did so with a heavy leaning toward either occult settings, esoteric symbolism, the supernatural & fantasy or all of these.

In this collection, we've interwoven fact and fiction; however, some of these non-fiction essays border on being unintentionally fantastical in nature. Two of the non-fictional pieces in this collection fall into this category; the essay on vampires and the longer piece about non-human inhabitants of the astral plane. At the time these pieces were written, the authors most certainly intended them as (*and they were originally read as*) much more serious articles than we see them as today. The co-mingling of fiction and non-fiction is very much how this written material would have been published at the time. For, it was common in the numerous occult periodicals of the day to have both types of articles, side-by-side without necessarily a clear indication of which ones were intended to be instructional and which ones were for entertainment. Two of the other non-fiction pieces which are included, fall more into the category of inspired prose or divine writing, while the one about Psychic Development is largely just straight-forwardly informative, at least from the author's perspective, anyway.

During the time period of publication for most of these essays, it was a common practice amongst esoteric writers, to straddle the fence between fiction and nonfiction. Often times writers would publish a tale that was clearly fictitious, while including real, living persons of the time, and claim that it was an authentic tale told to them, which proved the existence of real occult powers. This trope was sometimes used as a way to get their fiction published, in what would otherwise, primarily be non-fiction, occult periodicals. William Q. Judge and C. W. Leadbeater would both regularly employ this method, frequently going so far as to claim that Madame Blavatsky herself, no less, was even part of the so-called "real" story.

Similarly, sometimes, an occult writer of this era took a lot more liberties than one would today, with the inclusion of flowery prose, in their actual nonfiction. A case in point would probably be the regular inclusion of personal ghost stories (*or other supernatural creatures, be it vampires, fairy folk or some ill-defined spirits*) being used as anecdotal evidence to help prove the existence of the paranormal or of a specific individual's psychic or occult powers. Or, simply as a reinforcement that otherworldly events are always happening around us. It may sound like I just described the same thing twice, but I'm attempting to differentiate between the inclusion of a ghost in a fictional ghost-story and the story of a personal encounter with a ghost, which the author believes to have actually happened (*such as a friend or relative might relay to you*). Whether you, the reader, care to believe one story over the other, both or neither, these authors lived in a world where both real and fictional ghosts (*or other supernatural creatures*) could essentially live, side-by-side, without conflict.

On other occasions, these same writers didn't try to disguise their stories as non-fiction. Instead, they were upfront in letting their readers know that they simply wanted to spread their wings a bit and try their hand at some creative writing, while still sticking to familiar themes and areas of study they were interested in. Other writers still, such as was the case with Arthur Machen or Algernon Blackwood, were already well known to be primarily fiction writers, so the readers had come to expect mystical or supernatural undertones to their stories, without thinking too hard about if there might be some truth hiding just under the surface.

Enjoy then, this collection of occult writings, presented to you by Lamp of Trismegistus, and be sure to check out some of our other esoteric collections, as well. You can also download the audio versions of most of these titles from Audible, Amazon or Apple.

Cave of the Echoes

by Helena P. Blavatsky

A Strange but True Story*

(*) *This story is given from the narrative of an eye-witness, a Russian gentleman, very pious, and fully trustworthy. Moreover, the facts are copied from the police records of Polyarny. The eye-witness in question attributes it, of course, partly to divine interference and partly to the Evil One. — H. P. B.*

In one of the distant governments of the Russian empire, in a small town on the borders of Siberia, a mysterious tragedy occurred more than thirty years ago. About six versts from the little town of Polyarny, famous for the wild beauty of its scenery, and for the wealth of its inhabitants — generally proprietors of mines and of iron foundries — stood an aristocratic mansion. Its household consisted of the master, a rich old bachelor and his brother, who was a widower and the father of two sons and three daughters.

It was known that the proprietor, Mr. Izvertzoff, had adopted his brother's children, and, having formed an especial attachment for his eldest nephew, Nicolas, he made him the sole heir of his numerous estates.

Time rolled on. The uncle was getting old, the nephew was coming of age. Days and years had passed in monotonous serenity, when, on the hitherto clear horizon of the quiet family, appeared a cloud. On an unlucky day one of the nieces took it into her head to study the zither. The instrument being of purely Teutonic origin, and no teacher of it residing in the neighborhood, the indulgent uncle sent to St. Petersburg for both. After diligent search only one Professor could be found willing to trust himself in such close proximity to Siberia. It was an old German artist, who, sharing his affections equally between his instrument and a pretty blonde daughter, would part with neither. And thus it came to pass that, one fine morning, the old Professor arrived at the mansion, with his music box under one arm and his fair Munchen leaning on the other.

From that day the little cloud began growing rapidly; for every vibration of the melodious instrument found a responsive echo in the old bachelor's heart. Music awakens love, they say, and the work begun by the zither was completed by Munchen's blue eyes. At the expiration of six months the niece had become an expert zither player, and the uncle was desperately in love.

One morning, gathering his adopted family around him, he embraced them all very tenderly, promised to remember them in his will, and wound up by declaring his unalterable resolution to marry the blue-eyed Munchen. After this he fell upon their necks, and wept in silent rapture. The family, understanding that they were cheated out of the inheritance, also wept; but it was for another cause. Having thus wept, they consoled themselves and tried to rejoice, for the old gentleman was sincerely beloved by all. Not all of them rejoiced, though. Nicolas, who had himself been smitten to the heart by the pretty German, and who found himself defrauded at once of his belle and of his uncle's money, neither rejoiced nor consoled himself, but disappeared for a whole day.

Meanwhile, Mr. Izvertzoff had given orders to prepare his traveling carriage on the following day, and it was whispered that he was going to the chief town of the district, at some distance from his home, with the intention of altering his will. Though very wealthy, he had no superintendent on his estate, but kept his books himself. The same evening after supper, he was heard in his room, angrily scolding his servant, who had been in his service for over thirty years. This man, Ivan, was a native of northern Asia, from Kamtschatka; he had been brought up by the family in the Christian religion, and was thought to be very much attached to his master. A few days later, when the first tragic circumstance I am about to relate had brought all the police force to the spot, it was remembered that on that night Ivan was drunk; that his master, who had a horror of this vice, had paternally thrashed him, and turned him out of his room, and that Ivan had been seen reeling out of the door, and had been heard to mutter threats.

On the vast domain of Mr. Izvertzoff there was a curious cavern, which excited the curiosity of all who visited it. It exists to this day, and is well known to every inhabitant of Polyarny. A pine forest, commencing a few feet from the garden gate, climbs in steep terraces up a long range of rocky hills, which it covers with a broad belt of impenetrable vegetation. The grotto leading into the cavern, which is known as the "Cave of the Echoes," is situated about half a mile from the site of the mansion, from which it appears as a small excavation in the hillside, almost hidden by luxuriant plants, but not so completely as to prevent any person entering it from being readily seen from the terrace in front of the house. Entering the grotto, the explorer finds at the rear a narrow cleft; having passed through which he emerges into a lofty cavern, feebly lighted through fissures in the vaulted roof, fifty feet from the ground. The cavern itself is immense, and would easily hold between two and three thousand people. A part of it, in the days of Mr. Izvertzoff, was paved with flagstones, and was often used in the summer as a ballroom by picnic parties. Of an irregular oval, it gradually narrows into a broad corridor, which runs for several miles underground, opening here and there into other chambers, as large and lofty as the ballroom, but, unlike this, impassable otherwise than in a boat, as they are always full of water. These natural basins have the reputation of being unfathomable.

On the margin of the first of these is a small platform, with several mossy rustic seats arranged on it, and it is from this spot that the phenomenal echoes, which give the cavern its name, are heard in all their weirdness. A word pronounced in a whisper, or even a sigh, is caught up by endless mocking voices, and instead of diminishing in volume, as honest echoes do, the sound grows louder and louder at every successive repetition, until at last it bursts forth like the repercussion of a pistol shot, and recedes in a plaintive wail down the corridor.

On the day in question, Mr. Izvertzoff had mentioned his intention of having a dancing party in this cave on his wedding day, which he had fixed for an early date. On the following morning, while preparing for his drive, he was seen by his family entering the grotto, accompanied only by his Siberian servant. Half-an-hour later, Ivan returned to the mansion for a snuff-box which his master had forgotten in his room, and went back with it to the cave. An hour later the whole house was startled by his loud cries. Pale and dripping with water, Ivan rushed in like a madman, and declared that Mr. Izvertzoff was nowhere to be found in the cave. Thinking he had fallen into the lake, he had dived into the first basin in search of him and was nearly drowned himself.

The day passed in vain attempts to find the body. The police filled the house, and louder than the rest in his despair was Nicolas, the nephew, who had returned home only to meet the sad tidings.

A dark suspicion fell upon Ivan, the Siberian. He had been struck by his master the night before, and had been heard to swear revenge. He had accompanied him alone to the cave, and when his room was searched a box full of rich family jewelry, known to have been carefully kept in Mr. Izvertzoff's apartment, was found under Ivan's bedding. Vainly did the serf call God to witness that the box had been given to him in charge by his master himself, just before they proceeded to the cave; that it was the latter's purpose to have the jewelry reset, as he intended it for a wedding present to his bride; and that he, Ivan, would willingly give his own life to recall that of his master, if he knew him to be dead. No heed was paid to him, however, and he was arrested and thrown into prison, upon a charge of murder. There he was left, for under the Russian law a criminal cannot — at any rate, he could not in those days — be sentenced for a crime, however conclusive the circumstantial evidence, unless he confessed his guilt.

After a week had passed in useless search, the family arrayed themselves in deep mourning; and as the will as originally drawn remained without a codicil, the whole of the property passed into the hands of the nephew. The old teacher and his daughter bore this sudden reverse of fortune with true Germanic phlegm, and prepared to depart. Taking again his zither under one arm, the old man was about to lead away his Munchen by the other, when the nephew stopped him by offering himself as the fair damsel's husband in the place of his departed uncle. The change was found to be an agreeable one, and, without much ado, the young people were married.

Ten years rolled away, and we meet the happy family once more at the beginning of 1859. The fair Munchen had grown fat and vulgar. From the day of the old man's disappearance, Nicolas had become morose and retired in his habits, and many wondered at the change in him, for now he was never seen to smile. It seemed as if his only aim in life were to find out his uncle's murderer, or rather to bring Ivan to confess his guilt. But the man still persisted that he was innocent.

An only son had been born to the young couple, and a strange child it was. Small, delicate, and ever ailing, his frail life seemed to hang by a thread. When his features were in repose, his resemblance to his uncle was so striking that the members of the family often shrank from him in terror. It was the pale shriveled face of a man of sixty upon the shoulders of a child nine years old. He was never seen either to laugh or to play, but, perched in his high chair, would gravely sit there, folding his arms in a way peculiar to the late Mr. Izvertzoff; and thus he would remain for hours, drowsy and motionless. His nurses were often seen furtively crossing themselves at night, upon approaching him, and not one of them would consent to sleep alone with him in the nursery. His father's behavior towards him was still more strange. He seemed to love him passionately, and at the same time to hate him bitterly. He seldom embraced or caressed the child, but with livid cheek and staring eye, he would pass long hours watching him, as the child sat quietly in his corner, in his goblin-like, old-fashioned way.

The child had never left the estate, and few outside the family knew of his existence.

About the middle of July, a tall Hungarian traveler, preceded by a great reputation for eccentricity, wealth and mysterious powers, arrived at the town of Polyarny from the North, where, it was said, he had resided for many years. He settled in the little town, in company with a Shaman or South Siberian magician, on whom he was said to make mesmeric experiments. He gave dinners and parties, and invariably exhibited his Shaman, of whom he felt very proud, for the amusement of his guests. One day the notables of Polyarny made an unexpected invasion of the domains of Nicolas Izvertzoff, and requested the loan of his cave for an evening entertainment. Nicolas consented with great reluctance, and only after still greater hesitancy was he prevailed upon to join the party.

The first cavern and the platform beside the bottomless lake glittered with lights. Hundreds of flickering candles and torches, stuck in the clefts of the rocks, illuminated the place and drove the shadows from the mossy nooks and corners, where they had crouched undisturbed for many years. The stalactites on the walls sparkled brightly, and the sleeping echoes were suddenly awakened by a joyous confusion of laughter and conversation. The Shaman, who was never lost sight of by his friend and patron, sat in a corner, entranced as usual. Crouched on a projecting rock, about midway between the entrance and the water, with his lemon-yellow, wrinkled face, flat nose, and thin beard, he looked more like an ugly stone idol than a human being. Many of the company pressed around him and received correct answers to their questions, the Hungarian cheerfully submitting his mesmerized "subject" to cross-examination.

Suddenly one of the party, a lady, remarked that it was in that very cave that old Mr. Izvertzoff had so unaccountably disappeared ten years before. The foreigner appeared interested, and desired to learn more of the circumstances, so Nicolas was sought amid the crowd and led before the eager group. He was the host and he found it impossible to refuse the demanded narrative. He repeated the sad tale in a trembling voice, with a pallid cheek, and tears were seen glittering in his feverish eyes. The company were greatly affected, and encomiums upon the behavior of the loving nephew in honoring the memory of his uncle and benefactor were freely circulating in whispers, when suddenly the voice of Nicolas became choked, his eyes started from their sockets, and, with a suppressed groan, he staggered back. Every eye in the crowd followed with curiosity his haggard look, as it fell and remained riveted upon a weakened little face, that peeped from behind the back of the Hungarian.

"Where do you come from? Who brought you here, child?" gasped out Nicolas, as pale as death.

"I was in bed, papa; this man came to me, and brought me here in his arms," answered the boy simply, pointing to the Shaman, beside whom he stood upon the rock, and who, with his eyes closed, kept swaying himself to and fro like a living pendulum.

"That is very strange," remarked one of the guests, "for the man has never moved from his place."

"Good God! what an extraordinary resemblance!" muttered an old resident of the town, a friend of the lost man.

"You lie, child!" fiercely exclaimed the father. "Go to bed; this is no place for you."

"Come, come," interposed the Hungarian, with a strange expression on his face, and encircling with his arm the slender childish figure; "the little fellow has seen the double of my Shaman, which roams sometimes far away from his body, and has mistaken the phantom for the man himself. Let him remain with us for a while."

At these strange words the guests stared at each other in mute surprise, while some piously made the sign of the cross, spitting aside, presumably at the devil and all his works.

"By-the-bye," continued the Hungarian with a peculiar firmness of accent, and addressing the company rather than any one in particular; "why should we not try, with the help of my Shaman, to unravel the mystery hanging over the tragedy? Is the suspected party still lying in prison? What? he has not confessed up to now? This is surely very strange. But now we will learn the truth in a few minutes! Let all keep silent!"

He then approached the Tehuktchene, and immediately began his performance without so much as asking the consent of the master of the place. The latter stood rooted to the spot, as if petrified with horror, and unable to articulate a word. The suggestion met with general approbation, save from him; and the police inspector, Col. S-, especially approved of the idea.

"Ladies and gentlemen," said the mesmerizer in soft tones, "allow me for this once to proceed otherwise than in my general fashion. I will employ the method of native magic. It is more appropriate to this wild place, and far more effective as you will find, than our European method of mesmerization."

Without waiting for an answer, he drew from a bag that never left his person, first a small drum, and then two little phials — one full of fluid, the other empty. With the contents of the former he sprinkled the Shaman, who fell to trembling and nodding more violently than ever. The air was filled with the perfume of spicy odors, and the atmosphere itself seemed to become clearer. Then, to the horror of those present, he approached the Tibetan, and taking a miniature stiletto from his pocket, he plunged the sharp steel into the man's forearm, and drew blood from it, which he caught in the empty phial. When it was half filled, he pressed the orifice of the wound with his thumb, and stopped the flow of blood as easily as if he had corked a bottle, after which he sprinkled the blood over the little boy's head. He then suspended the drum from his neck, and, with two ivory drum-sticks, which were covered with magic signs and letters, he began beating a sort of reveille, to drum up the spirits, as he said.

The bystanders, half-shocked and half-terrified by these extraordinary proceedings, eagerly crowded around him, and for a few moments a dead silence reigned throughout the lofty cavern. Nicolas, with his face livid and corpse-like, stood speechless as before. The mesmerizer had placed himself between the Shaman and the platform, when he began slowly drumming. The first notes were muffled, and vibrated so softly in the air that they awakened no echo, but the Shaman quickened his pendulum-like motion and the child became restless. The drummer then began a slow chant, low, impressive and solemn.

As the unknown words issued from his lips, the flames of the candles and torches wavered and flickered, until they began dancing in rhythm with the chant. A cold wind came wheezing from the dark corridors beyond the water, leaving a plaintive echo in its trail. Then a sort of nebulous vapor, seeming to ooze from the rocky ground and walls, gathered about the Shaman and the boy. Around the latter the aura was silvery and transparent, but the cloud, which enveloped the former was red and sinister.

Approaching nearer to the platform the magician beat a louder roll upon the drum, and this time the echo caught it up with terrific effect! It reverberated near and far in incessant peals; one wail followed another louder and louder, until the thundering roar seemed the chorus of a thousand demon voices rising from the fathomless depths of the lake. The water itself, whose surface, illuminated by many lights, had previously been smooth as a sheet of glass, became suddenly agitated, as if a powerful gust of wind had swept over its unruffled face. Another chant, and a roll of the drum, and the mountain trembled to its foundation with the cannon-like peals, which rolled through the dark and distant corridors. The Shaman's body rose two yards in the air, and nodding and swaying, sat, self-suspended like an apparition. But the transformation which now occurred in the boy chilled everyone, as they speechlessly watched the scene. The silvery cloud about the boy now seemed to lift him, too, into the air; but, unlike the Shaman, his feet never left the ground. The child began to grow, as though the work of years was miraculously accomplished in a few seconds. He became tall and large, and his senile features grew older with the ageing of his body. A few more seconds, and the youthful form had entirely disappeared. It was totally absorbed in another individuality, and, to the horror of those present who had been familiar with his appearance, this individuality was that of old Mr. Izvertzoff, and on his temple was a large gaping wound, from which trickled great drops of blood.

This phantom moved towards Nicolas, till it stood directly in front of him, while he, with his hair standing erect, with the look of a madman gazed at his own son, transformed into his uncle. The sepulchral silence was broken by the Hungarian, who, addressing the child phantom, asked him, in solemn voice:

"In the name of the great Master, of Him who has all power, answer the truth, and nothing but the truth. Restless spirit, hast thou been lost by accident, or foully murdered?"

The specter's lips moved, but it was the echo which answered for them in lugubrious shouts: "Murdered! mur-der-ed!! murdered!!!"

"Where? How? By whom?" asked the conjuror.

The apparition pointed a finger at Nicolas and, without removing its gaze or lowering its arms, retreated backwards slowly towards the lake. At every step it took, the younger Izvertzoff, as if compelled by some irresistible fascination, advanced a step towards it, until the phantom reached the lake, and the next moment was seen gliding on its surface. It was a fearful, ghostly scene!

When he had come within two steps of the brink of the watery abyss, a violent convulsion ran through the frame of the guilty man. Flinging himself upon his knees, he clung to one of the rustic seats with a desperate clutch, and staring wildly, uttered a long piercing cry of agony. The phantom now remained motionless on the water, and bending his extended finger, slowly beckoned him to come. Crouched in abject terror, the wretched man shrieked until the cavern rang again and again: "I did not . . . No, I did not murder you!"

Then came a splash, and now it was the boy who was in the dark water, struggling for his life, in the middle of the lake, with the same motionless stern apparition brooding over him.

"Papa! papa! Save me . . . I am drowning!" . . . cried a piteous little voice amid the uproar of the mocking echoes.

"My boy!" shrieked Nicolas, in the accents of a maniac, springing to his feet. "My boy! Save him! Oh, save him! . . . Yes I confess . . . I am the murderer . . . It is I who killed him!"

Another splash, and the phantom disappeared. With a cry of horror the company rushed towards the platform; but their feet were suddenly rooted to the ground, as they saw amid the swirling eddies a whitish shapeless mass holding the murderer and the boy in tight embrace, and slowly sinking into the bottomless lake . . .

On the morning after these occurrences, when, after a sleepless night, some of the party visited the residence of the Hungarian gentleman, they found it closed and deserted. He and the Shaman had disappeared. Many are among the old inhabitants of Polyarny who remember him; the Police Inspector, Col. S-, dying a few years ago in the full assurance that the noble traveler was the devil. To add to the general consternation the Izvertzoff mansion took fire on that same night and was completely destroyed. The Archbishop performed the ceremony of exorcism, but the locality is considered accursed to this day. The Government investigated the facts, and ordered silence.

Modern Vampires

by Franz Hartmann

A class of phenomena which has given rise to many strange and horrible occurrences is that of vampirism, or the preying upon the vitality of a person and abstracting from him nervous force. This kind of vampirism we meet every day and are ourselves often subjected to it. We often meet people whose very presence draws upon our strength and causes fatigue. Sensitive, hysterical or mediumistic persons always vampirize each other. To magnetize, hypnotize or influence a person is a kind of obsession; to absorb the thought, magnetism or influence of another is a kind of vampirism, and there are persons who can live entirely upon the vitality of others.

I shall offer some evidence of this, followed by advice.

Firstly, I have already mentioned in a previous paper on "Meta thesis" in the *Occult Review* the case of the "wonder girl" at Radein, who for seven years lived without food or drink, being nevertheless in good health. Instead of taking food she with drew vitality from the children that were brought to her for the purpose of receiving her blessing. Some of these children sickened, some wasted away and died. She did not do this consciously and willingly; for she was a very pious person and, owing to her long fasting, even considered a saint. Many other persons of that kind are known in history; accounts of such some times appear in the papers, but they are soon hushed up, because our scientists cannot explain them; their science being still only superficially acquainted with certain natural laws. Still, popular opinion claims that it is not healthy for young children to sleep with old people in their beds, and medical science silently approves of this view.

Secondly, in the Bible it is claimed that when David grew old, a young girl was given to him to supply him with vitality, and not very many years ago certain institutions, based upon this principle, were existing in France. Young girls were supplied to old men or women as bedfellows. Usually the old person (*after having had to submit to certain precautionary measures*) had to sleep between two girls, a fair-haired and a dark one; for which privilege he had to pay a certain sum. All of these girls soon lost vitality; some of them died; and these establishments were finally closed by order of the police.

This is called "Vampirism among the living"; but there is another kind of vampirism; namely, vampirism exercised by black magic, or sorcery, and the vampirism of the grave.

Thirdly, of vampirism exercised by witchcraft, the following may serve as an instance:—

A miller at a nearby town hired a young man to labor in his mill. The boy was healthy and strong; but after a while he began to look pale and emaciated, and his strength grew less from day to day. The miller asked him about his ailment; but the boy pretended not to know. At last, however, he confessed to him that every night near midnight something heavy, of the shape of a large-sized egg, was pressing upon his breast, causing a distressing nightmare, and rendering him unable to breathe or to move. The miller thereupon watched at the bedside of the boy, and made him promise to give him a certain sign when he felt the presence of the vampire. The boy gave the sign, and the miller grasped with both hands that egg-shaped thing, which, although being invisible, seemed to the touch as if it were made of gelatin. He carried it to the chimney and threw it into the fire, and the boy, after that time, was troubled no more. This story has been told to me by a relative who lived at the said mill when this occurrence took place.

Fourthly, the following is an extract from one of the numerous letters concerning such subjects which I often receive :—

Dear Sir,—Permit me to ask your advice in regard to the following mysterious case: A woman in my neighborhood, a widow, is the mother of four children, of whom the two oldest ones are twins. One of these, a beautiful girl, is fearfully troubled by what seems to me a mysterious invisible something, which almost every night presses upon her breast, drawing the vitality out of her, the body of the child growing cold and rigid as a corpse. The vampire, or whatever it may be called, announces its coming by raps, moving of furniture and noises of various kinds. I may say that a year ago, shortly before the trouble began, the mother of the child had to dismiss a thieving servant woman, whereupon that woman pronounced a curse, and said she would be revenged upon the child. The child was taken to the hospital, where they said it was "hysteria"; but they could do no good. While she was at the hospital the noises at the residence continued, and the mother received pinches, which caused swellings that remained visible for several days. Thanking you in advance for your answer, sincerely Mr. M.

What defenses can be employed against these vampires?

There are two obstacles in the way of understanding the nature of such cases; namely, the ignorance of the fact that vitality is not a product of the cellular activity of the natural body; but, on the contrary, the vitality of the body is a manifestation of the activity of life, which is a power as universal as magnetism or electricity; and, furthermore, there is the ignorance of the fact that this power can be attracted and employed, unconsciously by the majority of people and consciously by those who are acquainted with its laws. I am often asked to advise some remedy against the influence of black magic or vampirism, and I know of no other than to restore the health of the body, and to render it thus impermeable to such influences. In regard to counteracting such influences, magic powers can be counter acted only by "magic," i.e. spiritual power. The best remedy, therefore, is the power of the true faith; namely, confidence in one's own divine self, by means of which a protective "astral" shell is formed around us, through which no evil influence can penetrate. By this means we may protect ourselves and even another, if we surround him with our aura. This power, however, is at the present time not in everybody's possession; those who can drive out demons are now as rarely to be found as at the time of Jesus of Nazareth; and it will probably be sometime before the healing by the power of the Holy Spirit will become generally practiced by the medical fraternity as a whole.

The vampires of the grave belong to another order; but such cases seem to be at present of very rare occurrence in civilized countries. They constitute a disgusting subject, which hardly needs to be discussed in this paper. Some such cases, where the astral body of the dead kept the physical body in the grave in a state of preservation by supplying it with vitality obtained by vampirizing the living, are reported in Blavatsky's *Isis Unveiled*. I myself have no experience in this line.

Ancient Sorceries

by Algernon Blackwood

Part I

There are, it would appear, certain wholly unremarkable persons, with none of the characteristics that invite adventure, who yet once or twice in the course of their smooth lives undergo an experience so strange that the world catches its breath—and looks the other way! And it was cases of this kind, perhaps, more than any other, that fell into the wide-spread net of John Silence, the psychic doctor, and, appealing to his deep humanity, to his patience, and to his great qualities of spiritual sympathy, led often to the revelation of problems of the strangest complexity, and of the profoundest possible human interest.

Matters that seemed almost too curious and fantastic for belief he loved to trace to their hidden sources. To unravel a tangle in the very soul of things—and to release a suffering human soul in the process—was with him a veritable passion. And the knots he untied were, indeed, after passing strange.

The world, of course, asks for some plausible basis to which it can attach credence—something it can, at least, pretend to explain. The adventurous type it can understand: such people carry about with them an adequate explanation of their exciting lives, and their characters obviously drive them into the circumstances which produce the adventures. It expects nothing else from them, and is satisfied. But dull, ordinary folk have no right to out-of-the-way experiences, and the world having been led to expect otherwise, is disappointed with them, not to say shocked. Its complacent judgment has been rudely disturbed.

"Such a thing happened to *that* man!" it cries— "a commonplace person like that! It is too absurd! There must be something wrong!"

Yet there could be no question that something did actually happen to little Arthur Vezin, something of the curious nature he described to Dr. Silence. Outwardly or inwardly, it happened beyond a doubt, and in spite of the jeers of his few friends who heard the tale, and observed wisely that "such a thing might perhaps have come to Iszard, that crack-brained Iszard, or to that odd fish Minski, but it could never have happened to commonplace little Vezin, who was fore-ordained to live and die according to scale."

But, whatever his method of death was, Vezin certainly did not "live according to scale" so far as this particular event in his otherwise uneventful life was concerned; and to hear him recount it, and watch his pale delicate features change, and hear his voice grow softer and more hushed as he proceeded, was to know the conviction that his halting words perhaps failed sometimes to convey. He lived the thing over again each time he told it. His whole personality became muffled in the recital. It subdued him more than ever, so that the tale became a lengthy apology for an experience that he deprecated. He appeared to excuse himself and ask your pardon for having dared to take part in so fantastic an episode. For little Vezin was a timid, gentle, sensitive soul, rarely able to assert himself, tender to man and beast, and almost constitutionally unable to say No, or to claim many things that should rightly have been his. His whole scheme of life seemed utterly remote from anything more exciting than missing a train or losing an umbrella on an omnibus. And when this curious event came upon him he was already more years beyond forty than his friends suspected or he cared to admit.

John Silence, who heard him speak of his experience more than once, said that he sometimes left out certain details and put in others; yet they were all obviously true. The whole scene was unforgettably cinematographed on to his mind. None of the details were imagined or invented. And when he told the story with them all complete, the effect was undeniable. His appealing brown eyes shone, and much of the charming personality, usually so carefully repressed, came forward and revealed itself. His modesty was always there, of course, but in the telling he forgot the present and allowed himself to appear almost vividly as he lived again in the past of his adventure.

He was on the way home when it happened, crossing northern France from some mountain trip or other where he buried himself solitary-wise every summer. He had nothing but an unregistered bag in the rack, and the train was jammed to suffocation, most of the passengers being unredeemed holiday English. He disliked them, not because they were his fellow-countrymen, but because they were noisy and obtrusive, obliterating with their big limbs and tweed clothing all the quieter tints of the day that brought him satisfaction and enabled him to melt into insignificance and forget that he was anybody. These English clashed about him like a brass band, making him feel vaguely that he ought to be more self-assertive and obstreperous, and that he did not claim insistently enough all kinds of things that he didn't want and that were really valueless, such as corner seats, windows up or down, and so forth.

So that he felt uncomfortable in the train, and wished the journey were over and he was back again living with his unmarried sister in Surbiton.

And when the train stopped for ten panting minutes at the little station in northern France, and he got out to stretch his legs on the platform, and saw to his dismay a further batch of the British Isles debouching from another train, it suddenly seemed impossible to him to continue the journey. Even *his* flabby soul revolted, and the idea of staying a night in the little town and going on next day by a slower, emptier train, flashed into his mind. The guard was already shouting *"en voiture"* and the corridor of his compartment was already packed when the thought came to him. And, for once, he acted with decision and rushed to snatch his bag.

Finding the corridor and steps impassable, he tapped at the window (for he had a corner seat) and begged the Frenchman who sat opposite to hand his luggage out to him, explaining in his wretched French that he intended to break the journey there. And this elderly Frenchman, he declared, gave him a look, half of warning, half of reproach, that to his dying day he could never forget; handed the bag through the window of the moving train; and at the same time poured into his ears a long sentence, spoken rapidly and low, of which he was able to comprehend only the last few words: "*à cause du sommeil et à cause des chats.*"

In reply to Dr. Silence, whose singular psychic acuteness at once seized upon this Frenchman as a vital point in the adventure, Vezin admitted that the man had impressed him favourably from the beginning, though without being able to explain why. They had sat facing one another during the four hours of the journey, and though no conversation had passed between them—Vezin was timid about his stuttering French—he confessed that his eyes were being continually drawn to his face, almost, he felt, to rudeness, and that each, by a dozen nameless little politenesses and attentions, had evinced the desire to be kind. The men liked each other and their personalities did not clash, or would not have clashed had they chanced to come to terms of acquaintance. The Frenchman, indeed, seemed to have exercised a silent protective influence over the insignificant little Englishman, and without words or gestures betrayed that he wished him well and would gladly have been of service to him.

"And this sentence that he hurled at you after the bag?" asked John Silence, smiling that peculiarly sympathetic smile that always melted the prejudices of his patient, "were you unable to follow it exactly?"

"It was so quick and low and vehement," explained Vezin, in his small voice, "that I missed practically the whole of it. I only caught the few words at the very end, because he spoke them so clearly, and his face was bent down out of the carriage window so near to mine."

" '*À cause du sommeil et à cause des chats*'? " repeated Dr. Silence, as though half speaking to himself.

"That's it exactly," said Vezin; "which, I take it, means something like 'because of sleep and because of the cats,' doesn't it?"

"Certainly, that's how I should translate it," the doctor observed shortly, evidently not wishing to interrupt more than necessary.

"And the rest of the sentence—all the first part I couldn't understand, I mean—was a warning not to do something—not to stop in the town, or at some particular place in the town, perhaps. That was the impression it made on me."

Then, of course, the train rushed off, and left Vezin standing on the platform alone and rather forlorn.

The little town climbed in straggling fashion up a sharp hill rising out of the plain at the back of the station, and was crowned by the twin towers of the ruined cathedral peeping over the summit. From the station itself it looked uninteresting and modern, but the fact was that the mediaeval position lay out of sight just beyond the crest. And once he reached the top and entered the old streets, he stepped clean out of modern life into a bygone century. The noise and bustle of the crowded train seemed days away. The spirit of this silent hill-town, remote from tourists and motor-cars, dreaming its own quiet life under the autumn sun, rose up and cast its spell upon him. Long before he recognized this spell he acted under it. He walked softly, almost on tiptoe, down the winding narrow streets where the gables all but met over his head, and he entered the doorway of the solitary inn with a deprecating and modest demeanor that was in itself an apology for intruding upon the place and disturbing its dream.

At first, however, Vezin said, he noticed very little of all this. The attempt at analysis came much later. What struck him then was only the delightful contrast of the silence and peace after the dust and noisy rattle of the train. He felt soothed and stroked like a cat.

"Like a cat, you said?" interrupted John Silence, quickly catching him up.

"Yes. At the very start I felt that." He laughed apologetically. "I felt as though the warmth and the stillness and the comfort made me purr. It seemed to be the general mood of the whole place—then."

The inn, a rambling ancient house, the atmosphere of the old coaching days still about it, apparently did not welcome him too warmly. He felt he was only tolerated, he said. But it was cheap and comfortable, and the delicious cup of afternoon tea he ordered at once made him feel really very pleased with himself for leaving the train in this bold, original way. For to him it had seemed bold and original. He felt something of a dog. His room, too, soothed him with its dark paneling and low irregular ceiling, and the long sloping passage that led to it seemed the natural pathway to a real Chamber of Sleep—a little dim cubby hole out of the world where noise could not enter. It looked upon the courtyard at the back. It was all very charming, and made him think of himself as dressed in very soft velvet somehow, and the floors seemed padded, the walls provided with cushions. The sounds of the streets could not penetrate there. It was an atmosphere of absolute rest that surrounded him.

On engaging the two-franc room he had interviewed the only person who seemed to be about that sleepy afternoon, an elderly waiter with Dundreary whiskers and a drowsy courtesy, who had ambled lazily towards him across the stone yard; but on coming downstairs again for a little promenade in the town before dinner he encountered the proprietress herself. She was a large woman whose hands, feet, and features seemed to swim towards him out of a sea of person. They emerged, so to speak. But she had great dark, vivacious eyes that counteracted the bulk of her body, and betrayed the fact that in reality she was both vigorous and alert. When he first caught sight of her, she was knitting in a low chair against the sunlight of the wall, and something at once made him see her as a great tabby cat, dozing, yet awake, heavily sleepy, and yet at the same time prepared for instantaneous action. A great mouser on the watch occurred to him.

She took him in with a single comprehensive glance that was polite without being cordial. Her neck, he noticed, was extraordinarily supple in spite of its proportions, for it turned so easily to follow him, and the head it carried bowed so very flexibly.

"But when she looked at me, you know," said Vezin, with that little apologetic smile in his brown eyes, and that faintly deprecating gesture of the shoulders that was characteristic of him, "the odd notion came to me that really she had intended to make quite a different movement, and that with a single bound she could have leaped at me across the width of that stone yard and pounced upon me like some huge cat upon a mouse."

He laughed a little soft laugh, and Dr. Silence made a note in his book without interrupting, while Vezin proceeded in a tone as though he feared he had already told too much and more than we could believe.

"Very soft, yet very active she was, for all her size and mass, and I felt she knew what I was doing even after I had passed and was behind her back. She spoke to me, and her voice was smooth and running. She asked if I had my luggage, and was comfortable in my room, and then added that dinner was at seven o'clock, and that they were very early people in this little country town. Clearly, she intended to convey that late hours were not encouraged."

Evidently, she contrived by voice and manner to give him the impression that here he would be "managed," that everything would be arranged and planned for him, and that he had nothing to do but fall into the groove and obey. No decided action or sharp personal effort would be looked for from him. It was the very reverse of the train. He walked quietly out into the street feeling soothed and peaceful. He realized that he was in a *milieu* that suited him and stroked him the right way. It was so much easier to be obedient. He began to purr again, and to feel that all the town purred with him.

About the streets of that little town he meandered gently, falling deeper and deeper into the spirit of repose that characterized it. With no special aim he wandered up and down, and to and fro. The September sunshine fell slantingly over the roofs. Down winding alleyways, fringed with tumbling gables and open casements, he caught fairylike glimpses of the great plain below, and of the meadows and yellow copses lying like a dream-map in the haze. The spell of the past held very potently here, he felt.

The streets were full of picturesquely garbed men and women, all busy enough, going their respective ways; but no one took any notice of him or turned to stare at his obviously English appearance. He was even able to forget that with his tourist appearance he was a false note in a charming picture, and he melted more and more into the scene, feeling delightfully insignificant and unimportant and unselfconscious. It was like becoming part of a softly colored dream which he did not even realize to be a dream.

On the eastern side the hill fell away more sharply, and the plain below ran off rather suddenly into a sea of gathering shadows in which the little patches of woodland looked like islands and the stubble fields like deep water. Here he strolled along the old ramparts of ancient fortifications that once had been formidable, but now were only vision-like with their charming mingling of broken grey walls and wayward vine and ivy. From the broad coping on which he sat for a moment, level with the rounded tops of clipped plane trees, he saw the esplanade far below lying in shadow. Here and there a yellow sunbeam crept in and lay upon the fallen yellow leaves, and from the height he looked down and saw that the townsfolk were walking to and fro in the cool of the evening. He could just hear the sound of their slow footfalls, and the murmur of their voices floated up to him through the gaps between the trees. The figures looked like shadows as he caught glimpses of their quiet movements far below.

He sat there for some time pondering, bathed in the waves of murmurs and half-lost echoes that rose to his ears, muffled by the leaves of the plane trees. The whole town, and the little hill out of which it grew as naturally as an ancient wood, seemed to him like a being lying there half asleep on the plain and crooning to itself as it dozed.

And, presently, as he sat lazily melting into its dream, a sound of horns and strings and wood instruments rose to his ears, and the town band began to play at the far end of the crowded terrace below to the accompaniment of a very soft, deep-throated drum. Vezin was very sensitive to music, knew about it intelligently, and had even ventured, unknown to his friends, upon the composition of quiet melodies with low-running chords which he played to himself with the soft pedal when no one was about. And this music floating up through the trees from an invisible and doubtless very picturesque band of the townspeople wholly charmed him. He recognized nothing that they played, and it sounded as though they were simply improvising without a conductor. No definitely marked time ran through the pieces, which ended and began oddly after the fashion of wind through an Aeolian harp. It was part of the place and scene, just as the dying sunlight and faintly breathing wind were part of the scene and hour, and the mellow notes of old-fashioned plaintive horns, pierced here and there by the sharper strings, all half smothered by the continuous booming of the deep drum, touched his soul with a curiously potent spell that was almost too engrossing to be quite pleasant.

There was a certain queer sense of bewitchment in it all. The music seemed to him oddly un-artificial. It made him think of trees swept by the wind, of night breezes singing among wires and chimney-stacks, or in the rigging of invisible ships; or—and the simile leaped up in his thoughts with a sudden sharpness of suggestion—a chorus of animals, of wild creatures, somewhere in desolate places of the world, crying and singing as animals will, to the moon. He could fancy he heard the wailing, half-human cries of cats upon the tiles at night, rising and falling with weird intervals of sound, and this music, muffled by distance and the trees, made him think of a queer company of these creatures on some roof far away in the sky, uttering their solemn music to one another and the moon in chorus.

It was, he felt at the time, a singular image to occur to him, yet it expressed his sensation pictorially better than anything else. The instruments played such impossibly odd intervals, and the crescendos and diminuendos were so very suggestive of cat-land on the tiles at night, rising swiftly, dropping without warning to deep notes again, and all in such strange confusion of discords and accords. But, at the same time a plaintive sweetness resulted on the whole, and the discords of these half-broken instruments were so singular that they did not distress his musical soul like fiddles out of tune.

He listened a long time, wholly surrendering himself as his character was, and then strolled homewards in the dusk as the air grew chilly.

"There was nothing to alarm?" put in Dr. Silence briefly.

"Absolutely nothing," said Vezin; "but you know it was all so fantastical and charming that my imagination was profoundly impressed. Perhaps, too," he continued, gently explanatory, "it was this stirring of my imagination that caused other impressions; for, as I walked back, the spell of the place began to steal over me in a dozen ways, though all intelligible ways. But there were other things I could not account for in the least, even then."

"Incidents, you mean?"

"Hardly incidents, I think. A lot of vivid sensations crowded themselves upon my mind and I could trace them to no causes. It was just after sunset and the tumbled old buildings traced magical outlines against an opalescent sky of gold and red. The dusk was running down the twisted streets. All round the hill the plain pressed in like a dim sea, its level rising with the darkness. The spell of this kind of scene, you know, can be very moving, and it was so that night. Yet I felt that what came to me had nothing directly to do with the mystery and wonder of the scene."

"Not merely the subtle transformations of the spirit that come with beauty," put in the doctor, noticing his hesitation.

"Exactly," Vezin went on, duly encouraged and no longer so fearful of our smiles at his expense. "The impressions came from somewhere else. For instance, down the busy main street where men and women were bustling home from work, shopping at stalls and barrows, idly gossiping in groups, and all the rest of it, I saw that I aroused no interest and that no one turned to stare at me as a foreigner and stranger. I was utterly ignored, and my presence among them excited no special interest or attention.

"And then, quite suddenly, it dawned upon me with conviction that all the time this indifference and inattention were merely feigned. Everybody as a matter of fact was watching me closely. Every movement I made was known and observed. Ignoring me was all a pretense—an elaborate pretense."

He paused a moment and looked at us to see if we were smiling, and then continued, reassured—

"It is useless to ask me how I noticed this, because I simply cannot explain it. But the discovery gave me something of a shock. Before I got back to the inn, however, another curious thing rose up strongly in my mind and forced my recognition of it as true. And this, too, I may as well say at once, was equally inexplicable to me. I mean I can only give you the fact, as fact it was to me."

The little man left his chair and stood on the mat before the fire. His diffidence lessened from now onwards, as he lost himself again in the magic of the old adventure. His eyes shone a little already as he talked.

"Well," he went on, his soft voice rising somewhat with his excitement, "I was in a shop when it came to me first—though the idea must have been at work for a long time subconsciously to appear in so complete a form all at once. I was buying socks, I think," he laughed, "and struggling with my dreadful French, when it struck me that the woman in the shop did not care two pins whether I bought anything or not. She was indifferent whether she made a sale or did not make a sale. She was only pretending to sell.

"This sounds a very small and fanciful incident to build upon what follows. But really it was not small. I mean it was the spark that lit the line of powder and ran along to the big blaze in my mind.

"For the whole town, I suddenly realized, was something other than I so far saw it. The real activities and interests of the people were elsewhere and otherwise than appeared. Their true lives lay somewhere out of sight behind the scenes. Their busy-ness was but the outward semblance that masked their actual purposes. They bought and sold, and ate and drank, and walked about the streets, yet all the while the main stream of their existence lay somewhere beyond my ken, underground, in secret places. In the shops and at the stalls they did not care whether I purchased their articles or not; at the inn, they were indifferent to my staying or going; their life lay remote from my own, springing from hidden, mysterious sources, coursing out of sight, unknown. It was all a great elaborate pretense, assumed possibly for my benefit, or possibly for purposes of their own. But the main current of their energies ran elsewhere. I almost felt as an unwelcome foreign substance might be expected to feel when it has found its way into the human system and the whole body organizes itself to eject it or to absorb it. The town was doing this very thing to me.

"This bizarre notion presented itself forcibly to my mind as I walked home to the inn, and I began busily to wonder wherein the true life of this town could lie and what were the actual interests and activities of its hidden life.

"And, now that my eyes were partly opened, I noticed other things too that puzzled me, first of which, I think, was the extraordinary silence of the whole place. Positively, the town was muffled. Although the streets were paved with cobbles the people moved about silently, softly, with padded feet, like cats. Nothing made noise. All was hushed, subdued, muted. The very voices were quiet, low-pitched like purring. Nothing clamorous, vehement or emphatic seemed able to live in the drowsy atmosphere of soft dreaming that soothed this little hill-town into its sleep. It was like the woman at the inn—an outward repose screening intense inner activity and purpose.

"Yet there was no sign of lethargy or sluggishness anywhere about it. The people were active and alert. Only a magical and uncanny softness lay over them all like a spell."

Vezin passed his hand across his eyes for a moment as though the memory had become very vivid. His voice had run off into a whisper so that we heard the last part with difficulty. He was telling a true thing obviously, yet something that he both liked and hated telling.

"I went back to the inn," he continued presently in a louder voice, "and dined. I felt a new strange world about me. My old world of reality receded. Here, whether I liked it or no, was something new and incomprehensible. I regretted having left the train so impulsively. An adventure was upon me, and I loathed adventures as foreign to my nature. Moreover, this was the beginning apparently of an adventure somewhere deep within me, in a region I could not check or measure, and a feeling of alarm mingled itself with my wonder—alarm for the stability of what I had for forty years recognized as my 'personality.'

"I went upstairs to bed, my mind teeming with thoughts that were unusual to me, and of rather a haunting description. By way of relief I kept thinking of that nice, prosaic noisy train and all those wholesome, blustering passengers. I almost wished I were with them again. But my dreams took me elsewhere. I dreamed of cats, and soft-moving creatures, and the silence of life in a dim muffled world beyond the senses."

Part II

Vezin stayed on from day to day, indefinitely, much longer than he had intended. He felt in a kind of dazed, somnolent condition. He did nothing in particular, but the place fascinated him and he could not decide to leave. Decisions were always very difficult for him and he sometimes wondered how he had ever brought himself to the point of leaving the train. It seemed as though someone else must have arranged it for him, and once or twice his thoughts ran to the swarthy Frenchman who had sat opposite. If only he could have understood that long sentence ending so strangely with "*à cause du sommeil et à cause des chats.*" He wondered what it all meant.

Meanwhile the hushed softness of the town held him prisoner and he sought in his muddling, gentle way to find out where the mystery lay, and what it was all about. But his limited French and his constitutional hatred of active investigation made it hard for him to buttonhole anybody and ask questions. He was content to observe, and watch, and remain negative.

The weather held on calm and hazy, and this just suited him. He wandered about the town till he knew every street and alley. The people suffered him to come and go without let or hindrance, though it became clearer to him every day that he was never free himself from observation. The town watched him as a cat watches a mouse. And he got no nearer to finding out what they were all so busy with or where the main stream of their activities lay. This remained hidden. The people were as soft and mysterious as cats.

But that he was continually under observation became more evident from day to day.

For instance, when he strolled to the end of the town and entered a little green public garden beneath the ramparts and seated himself upon one of the empty benches in the sun, he was quite alone—at first. Not another seat was occupied; the little park was empty, the paths deserted. Yet, within ten minutes of his coming, there must have been fully twenty persons scattered about him, some strolling aimlessly along the gravel walks, staring at the flowers, and others seated on the wooden benches enjoying the sun like himself. None of them appeared to take any notice of him; yet he understood quite well they had all come there to watch. They kept him under close observation. In the street they had seemed busy enough, hurrying upon various errands; yet these were suddenly all forgotten and they had nothing to do but loll and laze in the sun, their duties unremembered. Five minutes after he left, the garden was again deserted, the seats vacant. But in the crowded street it was the same thing again; he was never alone. He was ever in their thoughts.

By degrees, too, he began to see how it was he was so cleverly watched, yet without the appearance of it. The people did nothing *directly*. They behaved *obliquely*. He laughed in his mind as the thought thus clothed itself in words, but the phrase exactly described it. They looked at him from angles which naturally should have led their sight in another direction altogether. Their movements were oblique, too, so far as these concerned himself. The straight, direct thing was not their way evidently. They did nothing obviously. If he entered a shop to buy, the woman walked instantly away and busied herself with something at the farther end of the counter, though answering at once when he spoke, showing that she knew he was there and that this was only her way of attending to him. It was the fashion of the cat she followed. Even in the dining-room of the inn, the be-whiskered and courteous waiter, lithe and silent in all his movements, never seemed able to come straight to his table for an order or a dish. He came by zigzags, indirectly, vaguely, so that he appeared to be going to another table altogether, and only turned suddenly at the last moment, and was there beside him.

Vezin smiled curiously to himself as he described how he began to realize these things. Other tourists there were none in the hostel, but he recalled the figures of one or two old men, inhabitants, who took their *déjeuner* and dinner there, and remembered how fantastically they entered the room in similar fashion. First, they paused in the doorway, peering about the room, and then, after a temporary inspection, they came in, as it were, sideways, keeping close to the walls so that he wondered which table they were making for, and at the last minute making almost a little quick run to their particular seats. And again he thought of the ways and methods of cats.

Other small incidents, too, impressed him as all part of this queer, soft town with its muffled, indirect life, for the way some of the people appeared and disappeared with extraordinary swiftness puzzled him exceedingly. It may have been all perfectly natural, he knew, yet he could not make it out how the alleys swallowed them up and shot them forth in a second of time when there were no visible doorways or openings near enough to explain the phenomenon. Once he followed two elderly women who, he felt, had been particularly examining him from across the street—quite near the inn this was—and saw them turn the corner a few feet only in front of him. Yet when he sharply followed on their heels he saw nothing but an utterly deserted alley stretching in front of him with no sign of a living thing. And the only opening through which they could have escaped was a porch some fifty yards away, which not the swiftest human runner could have reached in time.

And in just such sudden fashion people appeared, when he never expected them. Once when he heard a great noise of fighting going on behind a low wall, and hurried up to see what was going on, what should he see but a group of girls and women engaged in vociferous conversation which instantly hushed itself to the normal whispering note of the town when his head appeared over the wall. And even then none of them turned to look at him directly, but slunk off with the most unaccountable rapidity into doors and sheds across the yard. And their voices, he thought, had sounded so like, so strangely like, the angry snarling of fighting animals, almost of cats.

The whole spirit of the town, however, continued to evade him as something elusive, protean, screened from the outer world, and at the same time intensely, genuinely vital; and, since he now formed part of its life, this concealment puzzled and irritated him; more—it began rather to frighten him.

Out of the mists that slowly gathered about his ordinary surface thoughts, there rose again the idea that the inhabitants were waiting for him to declare himself, to take an attitude, to do this, or to do that; and that when he had done so they in their turn would at length make some direct response, accepting or rejecting him. Yet the vital matter concerning which his decision was awaited came no nearer to him.

Once or twice he purposely followed little processions or groups of the citizens in order to find out, if possible, on what purpose they were bent; but they always discovered him in time and dwindled away, each individual going his or her own way. It was always the same: he never could learn what their main interest was. The cathedral was ever empty, the old church of St. Martin, at the other end of the town, deserted. They shopped because they had to, and not because they wished to. The booths stood neglected, the stalls unvisited, the little *cafés* desolate. Yet the streets were always full, the townsfolk ever on the bustle.

"Can it be," he thought to himself, yet with a deprecating laugh that he should have dared to think anything so odd, "can it be that these people are people of the twilight, that they live only at night their real life, and come out honestly only with the dusk? That during the day they make a sham though brave pretense, and after the sun is down their true life begins? Have they the souls of night-things, and is the whole blessed town in the hands of the cats?"

The fancy somehow electrified him with little shocks of shrinking and dismay. Yet, though he affected to laugh, he knew that he was beginning to feel more than uneasy, and that strange forces were tugging with a thousand invisible cords at the very center of his being. Something utterly remote from his ordinary life, something that had not waked for years, began faintly to stir in his soul, sending feelers abroad into his brain and heart, shaping queer thoughts and penetrating even into certain of his minor actions. Something exceedingly vital to himself, to his soul, hung in the balance.

And, always when he returned to the inn about the hour of sunset, he saw the figures of the townsfolk stealing through the dusk from their shop doors, moving sentry-wise to and fro at the corners of the streets, yet always vanishing silently like shadows at his near approach. And as the inn invariably closed its doors at ten o'clock he had never yet found the opportunity he rather half-heartedly sought to see for himself what account the town could give of itself at night.

"—*à cause du sommeil et à cause des chats*"—the words now rang in his ears more and more often, though still as yet without any definite meaning.

Moreover, something made him sleep like the dead.

Part III

It was, I think, on the fifth day—though in this detail his story sometimes varied—that he made a definite discovery which increased his alarm and brought him up to a rather sharp climax. Before that he had already noticed that a change was going forward and certain subtle transformations being brought about in his character which modified several of his minor habits. And he had affected to ignore them. Here, however, was something he could no longer ignore; and it startled him.

At the best of times he was never very positive, always negative rather, compliant and acquiescent; yet, when necessity arose he was capable of reasonably vigorous action and could take a strongish decision. The discovery he now made that brought him up with such a sharp turn was that this power had positively dwindled to nothing. He found it impossible to make up his mind. For, on this fifth day, he realized that he had stayed long enough in the town and that for reasons he could only vaguely define to himself it was wiser *and safer* that he should leave.

And he found that he could not leave!

This is difficult to describe in words, and it was more by gesture and the expression of his face that he conveyed to Dr. Silence the state of impotence he had reached. All this spying and watching, he said, had as it were, spun a net about his feet so that he was trapped and powerless to escape; he felt like a fly that had blundered into the intricacies of a great web; he was caught, imprisoned, and could not get away. It was a distressing sensation. A numbness had crept over his will till it had become almost incapable of decision. The mere thought of vigorous action—action towards escape—began to terrify him. All the currents of his life had turned inwards upon himself, striving to bring to the surface something that lay buried almost beyond reach, determined to force his recognition of something he had long forgotten—forgotten years upon years, centuries almost ago. It seemed as though a window deep within his being would presently open and reveal an entirely new world, yet somehow a world that was not unfamiliar. Beyond that, again, he fancied a great curtain hung; and when that too rolled up he would see still farther into this region and at last understand something of the secret life of these extraordinary people.

"Is this why they wait and watch?" he asked himself with rather a shaking heart, "for the time when I shall join them—or refuse to join them? Does the decision rest with me after all, and not with them?"

And it was at this point that the sinister character of the adventure first really declared itself, and he became genuinely alarmed. The stability of his rather fluid little personality was at stake, he felt, and something in his heart turned coward.

Why otherwise should he have suddenly taken to walking stealthily, silently, making as little sound as possible, forever looking behind him? Why else should he have moved almost on tiptoe about the passages of the practically deserted inn, and when he was abroad have found himself deliberately taking advantage of what cover presented itself? And why, if he was not afraid, should the wisdom of staying indoors after sundown have suddenly occurred to him as eminently desirable? Why, indeed?

And, when John Silence gently pressed him for an explanation of these things, he admitted apologetically that he had none to give.

"It was simply that I feared something might happen to me unless I kept a sharp look-out. I felt afraid. It was instinctive," was all he could say. "I got the impression that the whole town was after me—wanted me for something; and that if it got me I should lose myself, or at least the Self I knew, in some unfamiliar state of consciousness. But I am not a psychologist, you know," he added meekly, "and I cannot define it better than that."

It was while lounging in the courtyard half an hour before the evening meal that Vezin made this discovery, and he at once went upstairs to his quiet room at the end of the winding passage to think it over alone. In the yard it was empty enough, true, but there was always the possibility that the big woman whom he dreaded would come out of some door, with her pretense of knitting, to sit and watch him. This had happened several times, and he could not endure the sight of her. He still remembered his original fancy, bizarre though it was, that she would spring upon him the moment his back was turned and land with one single crushing leap upon his neck. Of course, it was nonsense, but then it haunted him, and once an idea begins to do that it ceases to be nonsense. It has clothed itself in reality.

He went upstairs accordingly. It was dusk, and the oil lamps had not yet been lit in the passages. He stumbled over the uneven surface of the ancient flooring, passing the dim outlines of doors along the corridor—doors that he had never once seen opened— rooms that seemed never occupied. He moved, as his habit now was, stealthily and on tiptoe.

Half-way down the last passage to his own chamber there was a sharp turn, and it was just here, while groping round the walls with outstretched hands, that his fingers touched something that was not wall—something that moved. It was soft and warm in texture, indescribably fragrant, and about the height of his shoulder; and he immediately thought of a furry, sweet-smelling kitten. The next minute he knew it was something quite different.

Instead of investigating, however,—his nerves must have been too overwrought for that, he said,—he shrank back as closely as possible against the wall on the other side. The thing, whatever it was, slipped past him with a sound of rustling and, retreating with light footsteps down the passage behind him, was gone. A breath of warm, scented air was wafted to his nostrils.

Vezin caught his breath for an instant and paused, stockstill, half leaning against the wall—and then almost ran down the remaining distance and entered his room with a rush, locking the door hurriedly behind him. Yet it was not fear that made him run: it was excitement, pleasurable excitement. His nerves were tingling, and a delicious glow made itself felt all over his body. In a flash it came to him that this was just what he had felt twenty-five years ago as a boy when he was in love for the first time. Warm currents of life ran all over him and mounted to his brain in a whirl of soft delight. His mood was suddenly become tender, melting, loving.

The room was quite dark, and he collapsed upon the sofa by the window, wondering what had happened to him and what it all meant. But the only thing he understood clearly in that instant was that something in him had swiftly, magically changed: he no longer wished to leave, or to argue with himself about leaving. The encounter in the passage-way had changed all that. The strange perfume of it still hung about him, bemusing his heart and mind. For he knew that it was a girl who had passed him, a girl's face that his fingers had brushed in the darkness, and he felt in some extraordinary way as though he had been actually kissed by her, kissed full upon the lips.

Trembling, he sat upon the sofa by the window and struggled to collect his thoughts. He was utterly unable to understand how the mere passing of a girl in the darkness of a narrow passage-way could communicate so electric a thrill to his whole being that he still shook with the sweetness of it. Yet, there it was! And he found it as useless to deny as to attempt analysis. Some ancient fire had entered his veins, and now ran coursing through his blood; and that he was forty-five instead of twenty did not matter one little jot. Out of all the inner turmoil and confusion emerged the one salient fact that the mere atmosphere, the merest casual touch, of this girl, unseen, unknown in the darkness, had been sufficient to stir dormant fires in the center of his heart, and rouse his whole being from a state of feeble sluggishness to one of tearing and tumultuous excitement.

After a time, however, the number of Vezin's years began to assert their cumulative power; he grew calmer, and when a knock came at length upon his door and he heard the waiter's voice suggesting that dinner was nearly over, he pulled himself together and slowly made his way downstairs into the dining-room.

Everyone looked up as he entered, for he was very late, but he took his customary seat in the far corner and began to eat. The trepidation was still in his nerves, but the fact that he had passed through the courtyard and hall without catching sight of a petticoat served to calm him a little. He ate so fast that he had almost caught up with the current stage of the table d'hôte, when a slight commotion in the room drew his attention.

His chair was so placed that the door and the greater portion of the long *salle à manger* were behind him, yet it was not necessary to turn round to know that the same person he had passed in the dark passage had now come into the room. He felt the presence long before he heard or saw any one. Then he became aware that the old men, the only other guests, were rising one by one in their places, and exchanging greetings with someone who passed among them from table to table. And when at length he turned with his heart beating furiously to ascertain for himself, he saw the form of a young girl, lithe and slim, moving down the center of the room and making straight for his own table in the corner. She moved wonderfully, with sinuous grace, like a young panther, and her approach filled him with such delicious bewilderment that he was utterly unable to tell at first what her face was like, or discover what it was about the whole presentment of the creature that filled him anew with trepidation and delight.

"Ah, Ma'mselle est de retour!" he heard the old waiter murmur at his side, and he was just able to take in that she was the daughter of the proprietress, when she was upon him, and he heard her voice. She was addressing him. Something of red lips he saw and laughing white teeth, and stray wisps of fine dark hair about the temples; but all the rest was a dream in which his own emotion rose like a thick cloud before his eyes and prevented his seeing accurately, or knowing exactly what he did. He was aware that she greeted him with a charming little bow; that her beautiful large eyes looked searchingly into his own; that the perfume he had noticed in the dark passage again assailed his nostrils, and that she was bending a little towards him and leaning with one hand on the table at this side. She was quite close to him—that was the chief thing he knew—explaining that she had been asking after the comfort of her mother's guests, and now was introducing herself to the latest arrival—himself.

"M'sieur has already been here a few days," he heard the waiter say; and then her own voice, sweet as singing, replied—

"Ah, but M'sieur is not going to leave us just yet, I hope. My mother is too old to look after the comfort of our guests properly, but now I am here I will remedy all that." She laughed deliciously. "M'sieur shall be well looked after."

Vezin, struggling with his emotion and desire to be polite, half rose to acknowledge the pretty speech, and to stammer some sort of reply, but as he did so his hand by chance touched her own that was resting upon the table, and a shock that was for all the world like a shock of electricity, passed from her skin into his body. His soul wavered and shook deep within him. He caught her eyes fixed upon his own with a look of most curious intentness, and the next moment he knew that he had sat down wordless again on his chair, that the girl was already half-way across the room, and that he was trying to eat his salad with a dessert-spoon and a knife.

Longing for her return, and yet dreading it, he gulped down the remainder of his dinner, and then went at once to his bedroom to be alone with his thoughts. This time the passages were lighted, and he suffered no exciting contretemps; yet the winding corridor was dim with shadows, and the last portion, from the bend of the walls onwards, seemed longer than he had ever known it. It ran downhill like the pathway on a mountain side, and as he tiptoed softly down it he felt that by rights it ought to have led him clean out of the house into the heart of a great forest. The world was singing with him. Strange fancies filled his brain, and once in the room, with the door securely locked, he did not light the candles, but sat by the open window thinking long, long thoughts that came unbidden in troops to his mind.

Part IV

This part of the story he told to Dr. Silence, without special coaxing, it is true, yet with much stammering embarrassment. He could not in the least understand, he said, how the girl had managed to affect him so profoundly, and even before he had set eyes upon her. For her mere proximity in the darkness had been sufficient to set him on fire. He knew nothing of enchantments, and for years had been a stranger to anything approaching tender relations with any member of the opposite sex, for he was encased in shyness, and realized his overwhelming defects only too well. Yet this bewitching young creature came to him deliberately. Her manner was unmistakable, and she sought him out on every possible occasion. Chaste and sweet she was undoubtedly, yet frankly inviting; and she won him utterly with the first glance of her shining eyes, even if she had not already done so in the dark merely by the magic of her invisible presence.

"You felt she was altogether wholesome and good!" queried the doctor. "You had no reaction of any sort—for instance, of alarm?"

Vezin looked up sharply with one of his inimitable little apologetic smiles. It was some time before he replied. The mere memory of the adventure had suffused his shy face with blushes, and his brown eyes sought the floor again before he answered.

"I don't think I can quite say that," he explained presently. "I acknowledged certain qualms, sitting up in my room afterwards. A conviction grew upon me that there was something about her— how shall I express it?—well, something unholy. It is not impurity in any sense, physical or mental, that I mean, but something quite indefinable that gave me a vague sensation of the creeps. She drew me, and at the same time repelled me, more than—than—"

He hesitated, blushing furiously, and unable to finish the sentence.

"Nothing like it has ever come to me before or since," he concluded, with lame confusion. "I suppose it was, as you suggested just now, something of an enchantment. At any rate, it was strong enough to make me feel that I would stay in that awful little haunted town for years if only I could see her every day, hear her voice, watch her wonderful movements, and sometimes, perhaps, touch her hand."

"Can you explain to me what you felt was the source of her power?" John Silence asked, looking purposely anywhere but at the narrator.

"I am surprised that you should ask me such a question," answered Vezin, with the nearest approach to dignity he could manage. "I think no man can describe to another convincingly wherein lies the magic of the woman who ensnares him. I certainly cannot. I can only say this slip of a girl bewitched me, and the mere knowledge that she was living and sleeping in the same house filled me with an extraordinary sense of delight.

"But there's one thing I can tell you," he went on earnestly, his eyes aglow, "namely, that she seemed to sum up and synthesize in herself all the strange hidden forces that operated so mysteriously in the town and its inhabitants. She had the silken movements of the panther, going smoothly, silently to and fro, and the same indirect, oblique methods as the townsfolk, screening, like them, secret purposes of her own—purposes that I was sure had *me* for their objective. She kept me, to my terror and delight, ceaselessly under observation, yet so carelessly, so consummately, that another man less sensitive, if I may say so"—he made a deprecating gesture—"or less prepared by what had gone before, would never have noticed it at all. She was always still, always reposeful, yet she seemed to be everywhere at once, so that I never could escape from her. I was continually meeting the stare and laughter of her great eyes, in the corners of the rooms, in the passages, calmly looking at me through the windows, or in the busiest parts of the public streets."

Their intimacy, it seems, grew very rapidly after this first encounter which had so violently disturbed the little man's equilibrium. He was naturally very prim, and prim folk live mostly in so small a world that anything violently unusual may shake them clean out of it, and they therefore instinctively distrust originality. But Vezin began to forget his primness after awhile. The girl was always modestly behaved, and as her mother's representative she naturally had to do with the guests in the hotel. It was not out of the way that a spirit of camaraderie should spring up. Besides, she was young, she was charmingly pretty, she was French, and—she obviously liked him.

At the same time, there was something indescribable—a certain indefinable atmosphere of other places, other times—that made him try hard to remain on his guard, and sometimes made him catch his breath with a sudden start. It was all rather like a delirious dream, half delight, half dread, he confided in a whisper to Dr. Silence; and more than once he hardly knew quite what he was doing or saying, as though he were driven forward by impulses he scarcely recognized as his own.

And though the thought of leaving presented itself again and again to his mind, it was each time with less insistence, so that he stayed on from day to day, becoming more and more a part of the sleepy life of this dreamy mediaeval town, losing more and more of his recognizable personality. Soon, he felt, the Curtain within would roll up with an awful rush, and he would find himself suddenly admitted into the secret purposes of the hidden life that lay behind it all. Only, by that time, he would have become transformed into an entirely different being.

And, meanwhile, he noticed various little signs of the intention to make his stay attractive to him: flowers in his bedroom, a more comfortable arm-chair in the corner, and even special little extra dishes on his private table in the dining-room. Conversations, too, with "Mademoiselle Ilsé" became more and more frequent and pleasant, and although they seldom travelled beyond the weather, or the details of the town, the girl, he noticed, was never in a hurry to bring them to an end, and often contrived to interject little odd sentences that he never properly understood, yet felt to be significant.

And it was these stray remarks, full of a meaning that evaded him, that pointed to some hidden purpose of her own and made him feel uneasy. They all had to do, he felt sure, with reasons for his staying on in the town indefinitely.

"And has M'sieur not even yet come to a decision?" she said softly in his ear, sitting beside him in the sunny yard before *déjeuner*, the acquaintance having progressed with significant rapidity. "Because, if it's so difficult, we must all try together to help him!"

The question startled him, following upon his own thoughts. It was spoken with a pretty laugh, and a stray bit of hair across one eye, as she turned and peered at him half roguishly. Possibly he did not quite understand the French of it, for her near presence always confused his small knowledge of the language distressingly. Yet the words, and her manner, and something else that lay behind it all in her mind, frightened him. It gave such point to his feeling that the town was waiting for him to make his mind up on some important matter.

At the same time, her voice, and the fact that she was there so close beside him in her soft dark dress, thrilled him inexpressibly.

"It is true I find it difficult to leave," he stammered, losing his way deliciously in the depths of her eyes, "and especially now that Mademoiselle Ilsé has come."

He was surprised at the success of his sentence, and quite delighted with the little gallantry of it. But at the same time he could have bitten his tongue off for having said it.

"Then after all you like our little town, or you would not be pleased to stay on," she said, ignoring the compliment.

"I am enchanted with it, and enchanted with you," he cried, feeling that his tongue was somehow slipping beyond the control of

55

his brain. And he was on the verge of saying all manner of other things of the wildest description, when the girl sprang lightly up from her chair beside him, and made to go.

"It is *soupe à l'onion* to-day!" she cried, laughing back at him through the sunlight, "and I must go and see about it. Otherwise, you know, M'sieur will not enjoy his dinner, and then, perhaps, he will leave us!"

He watched her cross the courtyard, moving with all the grace and lightness of the feline race, and her simple black dress clothed her, he thought, exactly like the fur of the same supple species. She turned once to laugh at him from the porch with the glass door, and then stopped a moment to speak to her mother, who sat knitting as usual in her corner seat just inside the hall-way.

But how was it, then, that the moment his eye fell upon this ungainly woman, the pair of them appeared suddenly as other than they were? Whence came that transforming dignity and sense of power that enveloped them both as by magic? What was it about that massive woman that made her appear instantly regal, and set her on a throne in some dark and dreadful scenery, wielding a scepter over the red glare of some tempestuous orgy? And why did this slender stripling of a girl, graceful as a willow, lithe as a young leopard, assume suddenly an air of sinister majesty, and move with flame and smoke about her head, and the darkness of night beneath her feet?

Vezin caught his breath and sat there transfixed. Then, almost simultaneously with its appearance, the queer notion vanished again, and the sunlight of day caught them both, and he heard her laughing to her mother about the *soupe à l'onion*, and saw her glancing back at him over her dear little shoulder with a smile that made him think of a dew-kissed rose bending lightly before summer airs.

And, indeed, the onion soup was particularly excellent that day, because he saw another cover laid at his small table, and, with fluttering heart, heard the waiter murmur by way of explanation that

"Ma'mselle Ilsé would honour M'sieur to-day at *déjeuner*, as her custom sometimes is with her mother's guests."

So actually she sat by him all through that delirious meal, talking quietly to him in easy French, seeing that he was well looked after, mixing the salad-dressing, and even helping him with her own hand. And, later in the afternoon, while he was smoking in the courtyard, longing for a sight of her as soon as her duties were done, she came again to his side, and when he rose to meet her, she stood facing him a moment, full of a perplexing sweet shyness before she spoke—

"My mother thinks you ought to know more of the beauties of our little town, and *I* think so too! Would M'sieur like me to be his guide, perhaps? I can show him everything, for our family has lived here for many generations."

She had him by the hand, indeed, before he could find a single word to express his pleasure, and led him, all unresisting, out into the street, yet in such a way that it seemed perfectly natural she should do so, and without the faintest suggestion of boldness or immodesty. Her face glowed with the pleasure and interest of it, and with her short dress and tumbled hair she looked every bit the charming child of seventeen that she was, innocent and playful, proud of her native town, and alive beyond her years to the sense of its ancient beauty.

So they went over the town together, and she showed him what she considered its chief interest: the tumble-down old house where her forebears had lived; the somber, aristocratic-looking mansion where her mother's family dwelt for centuries, and the ancient market-place where several hundred years before the witches had been burnt by the score. She kept up a lively running stream of talk about it all, of which he understood not a fiftieth part as he trudged along by her side, cursing his forty-five years and feeling all the yearnings of his early manhood revive and jeer at him. And, as she talked, England and Surbiton seemed very far away indeed, almost in another age of the world's history. Her voice touched something immeasurably old in him, something that slept deep. It lulled the surface parts of his consciousness to sleep, allowing what was far more ancient to awaken. Like the town, with its elaborate pretense of modern active life, the upper layers of his being became dulled, soothed, muffled, and what lay underneath began to stir in its sleep. That big Curtain swayed a little to and fro. Presently it might lift altogether....

He began to understand a little better at last. The mood of the town was reproducing itself in him. In proportion as his ordinary external-self became muffled, that inner secret life, that was far more real and vital, asserted itself. And this girl was surely the high-priestess of it all, the chief instrument of its accomplishment. New thoughts, with new interpretations, flooded his mind as she walked beside him through the winding streets, while the picturesque old gabled town, softly colored in the sunset, had never appeared to him so wholly wonderful and seductive.

And only one curious incident came to disturb and puzzle him, slight in itself, but utterly inexplicable, bringing white terror into the child's face and a scream to her laughing lips. He had merely pointed to a column of blue smoke that rose from the burning autumn leaves and made a picture against the red roofs, and had then run to the wall and called her to his side to watch the flames shooting here and there through the heap of rubbish. Yet, at the sight of it, as though taken by surprise, her face had altered dreadfully, and she had turned and run like the wind, calling out wild sentences to him as she ran, of which he had not understood a single word, except that the fire apparently frightened her, and she wanted to get quickly away from it, and to get him away too.

Yet five minutes later she was as calm and happy again as though nothing had happened to alarm or waken troubled thoughts in her, and they had both forgotten the incident.

They were leaning over the ruined ramparts together listening to the weird music of the band as he had heard it the first day of his arrival. It moved him again profoundly as it had done before, and somehow he managed to find his tongue and his best French. The girl leaned across the stones close beside him. No one was about. Driven by some remorseless engine within he began to stammer something—he hardly knew what—of his strange admiration for her. Almost at the first word she sprang lightly off the wall and came up smiling in front of him, just touching his knees as he sat there. She was hatless as usual, and the sun caught her hair and one side of her cheek and throat.

"Oh, I'm so glad!" she cried, clapping her little hands softly in his face, "so very glad, because that means that if you like me you must also like what I do, and what I belong to."

Already he regretted bitterly having lost control of himself. Something in the phrasing of her sentence chilled him. He knew the fear of embarking upon an unknown and dangerous sea.

"You will take part in our real life, I mean," she added softly, with an indescribable coaxing of manner, as though she noticed his shrinking. "You will come back to us."

Already this slip of a child seemed to dominate him; he felt her power coming over him more and more; something emanated from her that stole over his senses and made him aware that her personality, for all its simple grace, held forces that were stately, imposing, august. He saw her again moving through smoke and flame amid broken and tempestuous scenery, alarmingly strong, her terrible mother by her side. Dimly this shone through her smile and appearance of charming innocence.

"You will, I know," she repeated, holding him with her eyes.

They were quite alone up there on the ramparts, and the sensation that she was overmastering him stirred a wild sensuousness in his blood. The mingled abandon and reserve in her attracted him furiously, and all of him that was man rose up and resisted the creeping influence, at the same time acclaiming it with the full delight of his forgotten youth. An irresistible desire came to him to question her, to summon what still remained to him of his own little personality in an effort to retain the right to his normal self.

The girl had grown quiet again, and was now leaning on the broad wall close beside him, gazing out across the darkening plain, her elbows on the coping, motionless as a figure carved in stone. He took his courage in both hands.

"Tell me, Ilsé," he said, unconsciously imitating her own purring softness of voice, yet aware that he was utterly in earnest, "what is the meaning of this town, and what is this real life you speak of? And why is it that the people watch me from morning to night? Tell me what it all means? And, tell me," he added more quickly with passion in his voice, "what you really are—yourself?"

She turned her head and looked at him through half-closed eyelids, her growing inner excitement betraying itself by the faint color that ran like a shadow across her face.

"It seems to me,"—he faltered oddly under her gaze— "that I have some right to know—"

Suddenly she opened her eyes to the full. "You love me, then?" she asked softly.

"I swear," he cried impetuously, moved as by the force of a rising tide, "I never felt before—I have never known any other girl who—"

"Then you *have* the right to know," she calmly interrupted his confused confession, "for love shares all secrets."

She paused, and a thrill like fire ran swiftly through him. Her words lifted him off the earth, and he felt a radiant happiness, followed almost the same instant in horrible contrast by the thought of death. He became aware that she had turned her eyes upon his own and was speaking again.

"The real life I speak of," she whispered, "is the old, old life within, the life of long ago, the life to which you, too, once belonged, and to which you still belong."

A faint wave of memory troubled the deeps of his soul as her low voice sank into him. What she was saying he knew instinctively to be true, even though he could not as yet understand its full purport. His present life seemed slipping from him as he listened, merging his personality in one that was far older and greater. It was this loss of his present self that brought to him the thought of death.

"You came here," she went on, "with the purpose of seeking it, and the people felt your presence and are waiting to know what you decide, whether you will leave them without having found it, or whether—"

Her eyes remained fixed upon his own, but her face began to change, growing larger and darker with an expression of age.

"It is their thoughts constantly playing about your soul that makes you feel they watch you. They do not watch you with their eyes. The purposes of their inner life are calling to you, seeking to claim you. You were all part of the same life long, long ago, and now they want you back again among them."

Vezin's timid heart sank with dread as he listened; but the girl's eyes held him with a net of joy so that he had no wish to escape. She fascinated him, as it were, clean out of his normal self.

"Alone, however, the people could never have caught and held you," she resumed. "The motive force was not strong enough; it has faded through all these years. But I"—she paused a moment and looked at him with complete confidence in her splendid eyes— "I possess the spell to conquer you and hold you: the spell of old love. I can win you back again and make you live the old life with me, for the force of the ancient tie between us, if I choose to use it, is irresistible. And I do choose to use it. I still want you. And you, dear soul of my dim past"—she pressed closer to him so that her breath passed across his eyes, and her voice positively sang— "I mean to have you, for you love me and are utterly at my mercy."

Vezin heard, and yet did not hear; understood, yet did not understand. He had passed into a condition of exaltation. The world was beneath his feet, made of music and flowers, and he was flying somewhere far above it through the sunshine of pure delight. He was breathless and giddy with the wonder of her words. They intoxicated him. And, still, the terror of it all, the dreadful thought of death, pressed ever behind her sentences. For flames shot through her voice out of black smoke and licked at his soul.

And they communicated with one another, it seemed to him, by a process of swift telepathy, for his French could never have compassed all he said to her. Yet she understood perfectly, and what she said to him was like the recital of verses long since known. And the mingled pain and sweetness of it as he listened were almost more than his little soul could hold.

"Yet I came here wholly by chance—" he heard himself saying.

"No," she cried with passion, "you came here because I called to you. I have called to you for years, and you came with the whole force of the past behind you. You had to come, for I own you, and I claim you."

She rose again and moved closer, looking at him with a certain insolence in the face—the insolence of power.

The sun had set behind the towers of the old cathedral and the darkness rose up from the plain and enveloped them. The music of the band had ceased. The leaves of the plane trees hung motionless, but the chill of the autumn evening rose about them and made Vezin shiver. There was no sound but the sound of their voices and the occasional soft rustle of the girl's dress. He could hear the blood rushing in his ears. He scarcely realized where he was or what he was doing. Some terrible magic of the imagination drew him deeply down into the tombs of his own being, telling him in no unfaltering voice that her words shadowed forth the truth. And this simple little French maid, speaking beside him with so strange authority, he saw curiously alter into quite another being. As he stared into her eyes, the picture in his mind grew and lived, dressing itself vividly to his inner vision with a degree of reality he was compelled to acknowledge. As once before, he saw her tall and stately, moving through wild and broken scenery of forests and mountain caverns, the glare of flames behind her head and clouds of shifting smoke about her feet. Dark leaves encircled her hair, flying loosely in the wind, and her limbs shone through the merest rags of clothing. Others were about her, too, and ardent eyes on all sides cast delirious glances upon her, but her own eyes were always for One only, one whom she held by the hand. For she was leading the dance in some tempestuous orgy to the music of chanting voices, and the dance she led circled about a great and awful Figure on a throne, brooding over the scene through lurid vapors, while innumerable other wild faces and forms crowded furiously about her in the dance. But the one she held by the hand he knew to be himself, and the monstrous shape upon the throne he knew to be her mother.

The vision rose within him, rushing to him down the long years of buried time, crying aloud to him with the voice of memory reawakened.... And then the scene faded away and he saw the clear circle of the girl's eyes gazing steadfastly into his own, and she became once more the pretty little daughter of the innkeeper, and he found his voice again.

"And you," he whispered tremblingly— "you child of visions and enchantment, how is it that you so bewitch me that I loved you even before I saw?"

She drew herself up beside him with an air of rare dignity.

"The call of the Past," she said; "and besides," she added proudly, "in the real life I am a princess—"

"A princess!" he cried.

"—and my mother is a queen!"

At this, little Vezin utterly lost his head. Delight tore at his heart and swept him into sheer ecstasy. To hear that sweet singing voice, and to see those adorable little lips utter such things, upset his balance beyond all hope of control. He took her in his arms and covered her unresisting face with kisses.

But even while he did so, and while the hot passion swept him, he felt that she was soft and loathsome, and that her answering kisses stained his very soul.... And when, presently, she had freed herself and vanished into the darkness, he stood there, leaning against the wall in a state of collapse, creeping with horror from the touch of her yielding body, and inwardly raging at the weakness that he already dimly realized must prove his undoing.

And from the shadows of the old buildings into which she disappeared there rose in the stillness of the night a singular, long-drawn cry, which at first he took for laughter, but which later he was sure he recognized as the almost human wailing of a cat.

Part V

For a long time Vezin leant there against the wall, alone with his surging thoughts and emotions. He understood at length that he had done the one thing necessary to call down upon him the whole force of this ancient Past. For in those passionate kisses he had acknowledged the tie of olden days, and had revived it. And the memory of that soft impalpable caress in the darkness of the inn corridor came back to him with a shudder. The girl had first mastered him, and then led him to the one act that was necessary for her purpose. He had been waylaid, after the lapse of centuries—caught, and conquered.

Dimly he realized this, and sought to make plans for his escape. But, for the moment at any rate, he was powerless to manage his thoughts or will, for the sweet, fantastic madness of the whole adventure mounted to his brain like a spell, and he gloried in the feeling that he was utterly enchanted and moving in a world so much larger and wilder than the one he had ever been accustomed to.

The moon, pale and enormous, was just rising over the sea-like plain, when at last he rose to go. Her slanting rays drew all the houses into new perspective, so that their roofs, already glistening with dew, seemed to stretch much higher into the sky than usual, and their gables and quaint old towers lay far away in its purple reaches.

The cathedral appeared unreal in a silver mist. He moved softly, keeping to the shadows; but the streets were all deserted and very silent; the doors were closed, the shutters fastened. Not a soul was astir. The hush of night lay over everything; it was like a town of the dead, a churchyard with gigantic and grotesque tombstones.

Wondering where all the busy life of the day had so utterly disappeared to, he made his way to a back door that entered the inn by means of the stables, thinking thus to reach his room unobserved. He reached the courtyard safely and crossed it by keeping close to the shadow of the wall. He sidled down it, mincing along on tiptoe, just as the old men did when they entered the *salle à manger*. He was horrified to find himself doing this instinctively. A strange impulse came to him, catching him somehow in the center of his body—an impulse to drop upon all fours and run swiftly and silently. He glanced upwards and the idea came to him to leap up upon his window-sill overhead instead of going round by the stairs. This occurred to him as the easiest, and most natural way. It was like the beginning of some horrible transformation of himself into something else. He was fearfully strung up.

The moon was higher now, and the shadows very dark along the side of the street where he moved. He kept among the deepest of them, and reached the porch with the glass doors.

But here there was light; the inmates, unfortunately, were still about. Hoping to slip across the hall unobserved and reach the stairs, he opened the door carefully and stole in. Then he saw that the hall was not empty. A large dark thing lay against the wall on his left. At first he thought it must be household articles. Then it moved, and he thought it was an immense cat, distorted in some way by the play of light and shadow. Then it rose straight up before him and he saw that it was the proprietress.

What she had been doing in this position he could only venture a dreadful guess, but the moment she stood up and faced him he was aware of some terrible dignity clothing her about that instantly recalled the girl's strange saying that she was a queen. Huge and sinister she stood there under the little oil lamp; alone with him in the empty hall. Awe stirred in his heart, and the roots of some ancient fear. He felt that he must bow to her and make some kind of obeisance. The impulse was fierce and irresistible, as of long habit. He glanced quickly about him. There was no one there. Then he deliberately inclined his head toward her. He bowed.

"Enfin! M'sieur s'est donc décidé. C'est bien alors. J'en suis contente."

Her words came to him sonorously as through a great open space.

Then the great figure came suddenly across the flagged hall at him and seized his trembling hands. Some overpowering force moved with her and caught him.

"On pourrait faire un p'tit tour ensemble, n'est-ce pas? Nous y allons cette nuit et il faut s'exercer un peu d'avance pour cela. Ilsé, Ilsé, viens donc ici. Viens vite!"

And she whirled him round in the opening steps of some dance that seemed oddly and horribly familiar. They made no sound on the stones, this strangely assorted couple. It was all soft and stealthy. And presently, when the air seemed to thicken like smoke, and a red glare as of flame shot through it, he was aware that some one else had joined them and that his hand the mother had released was now tightly held by the daughter. Ilsé had come in answer to the call, and he saw her with leaves of vervain twined in her dark hair, clothed in tattered vestiges of some curious garment, beautiful as the night, and horribly, odiously, loathsomely seductive.

"To the Sabbath! to the Sabbath!" they cried. "On to the Witches' Sabbath!"

Up and down that narrow hall they danced, the women on each side of him, to the wildest measure he had ever imagined, yet which he dimly, dreadfully remembered, till the lamp on the wall flickered and went out, and they were left in total darkness. And the devil woke in his heart with a thousand vile suggestions and made him afraid.

Suddenly they released his hands and he heard the voice of the mother cry that it was time, and they must go. Which way they went he did not pause to see. He only realized that he was free, and he blundered through the darkness till he found the stairs and then tore up them to his room as though all hell was at his heels.

He flung himself on the sofa, with his face in his hands, and groaned. Swiftly reviewing a dozen ways of immediate escape, all equally impossible, he finally decided that the only thing to do for the moment was to sit quiet and wait. He must see what was going to happen. At least in the privacy of his own bedroom he would be fairly safe. The door was locked. He crossed over and softly opened the window which gave upon the courtyard and also permitted a partial view of the hall through the glass doors.

As he did so the hum and murmur of a great activity reached his ears from the streets beyond—the sound of footsteps and voices muffled by distance. He leaned out cautiously and listened. The moonlight was clear and strong now, but his own window was in shadow, the silver disc being still behind the house. It came to him irresistibly that the inhabitants of the town, who a little while before had all been invisible behind closed doors, were now issuing forth, busy upon some secret and unholy errand. He listened intently.

At first everything about him was silent, but soon he became aware of movements going on in the house itself. Rustlings and cheepings came to him across that still, moonlit yard. A concourse of living beings sent the hum of their activity into the night. Things were on the move everywhere. A biting, pungent odour rose through the air, coming he knew not whence. Presently his eyes became glued to the windows of the opposite wall where the moonshine fell in a soft blaze. The roof overhead, and behind him, was reflected clearly in the panes of glass, and he saw the outlines of dark bodies moving with long footsteps over the tiles and along the coping. They passed swiftly and silently, shaped like immense cats, in an endless procession across the pictured glass, and then appeared to leap down to a lower level where he lost sight of them. He just caught the soft thudding of their leaps. Sometimes their shadows fell upon the white wall opposite, and then he could not make out whether they were the shadows of human beings or of cats. They seemed to change swiftly from one to the other. The transformation looked horribly real, for they leaped like human beings, yet changed swiftly in the air immediately afterwards, and dropped like animals.

The yard, too, beneath him, was now alive with the creeping movements of dark forms all stealthily drawing towards the porch with the glass doors. They kept so closely to the wall that he could not determine their actual shape, but when he saw that they passed on to the great congregation that was gathering in the hall, he understood that these were the creatures whose leaping shadows he had first seen reflected in the windowpanes opposite. They were coming from all parts of the town, reaching the appointed meeting-place across the roofs and tiles, and springing from level to level till they came to the yard.

Then a new sound caught his ear, and he saw that the windows all about him were being softly opened, and that to each window came a face. A moment later figures began dropping hurriedly down into the yard. And these figures, as they lowered themselves down from the windows, were human, he saw; but once safely in the yard they fell upon all fours and changed in the swiftest possible second into—cats—huge, silent cats. They ran in streams to join the main body in the hall beyond.

So, after all, the rooms in the house had not been empty and unoccupied.

Moreover, what he saw no longer filled him with amazement. For he remembered it all. It was familiar. It had all happened before just so, hundreds of times, and he himself had taken part in it and known the wild madness of it all. The outline of the old building changed, the yard grew larger, and he seemed to be staring down upon it from a much greater height through smoky vapours. And, as he looked, half remembering, the old pains of long ago, fierce and sweet, furiously assailed him, and the blood stirred horribly as he heard the Call of the Dance again in his heart and tasted the ancient magic of Ilsé whirling by his side.

Suddenly he started back. A great lithe cat had leaped softly up from the shadows below on to the sill close to his face, and was staring fixedly at him with the eyes of a human. "Come," it seemed to say, "come with us to the Dance! Change as of old! Transform yourself swiftly and come!" Only too well he understood the creature's soundless call.

It was gone again in a flash with scarcely a sound of its padded feet on the stones, and then others dropped by the score down the side of the house, past his very eyes, all changing as they fell and darting away rapidly, softly, towards the gathering point. And again he felt the dreadful desire to do likewise; to murmur the old incantation, and then drop upon hands and knees and run swiftly for the great flying leap into the air. Oh, how the passion of it rose within him like a flood, twisting his very entrails, sending his heart's desire flaming forth into the night for the old, old Dance of the Sorcerers at the Witches' Sabbath! The whirl of the stars was about him; once more he met the magic of the moon. The power of the wind, rushing from precipice and forest, leaping from cliff to cliff across the valleys, tore him away.... He heard the cries of the dancers and their wild laughter, and with this savage girl in his embrace he danced furiously about the dim Throne where sat the Figure with the scepter of majesty....

Then, suddenly, all became hushed and still, and the fever died down a little in his heart. The calm moonlight flooded a courtyard empty and deserted. They had started. The procession was off into the sky. And he was left behind—alone.

Vezin tiptoed softly across the room and unlocked the door. The murmur from the streets, growing momentarily as he advanced, met his ears. He made his way with the utmost caution down the corridor. At the head of the stairs he paused and listened. Below him, the hall where they had gathered was dark and still, but through opened doors and windows on the far side of the building came the sound of a great throng moving farther and farther into the distance.

He made his way down the creaking wooden stairs, dreading yet longing to meet some straggler who should point the way, but finding no one; across the dark hall, so lately thronged with living, moving things, and out through the opened front doors into the street. He could not believe that he was really left behind, really forgotten, that he had been purposely permitted to escape. It perplexed him.

Nervously he peered about him, and up and down the street; then, seeing nothing, advanced slowly down the pavement.

The whole town, as he went, showed itself empty and deserted, as though a great wind had blown everything alive out of it. The doors and windows of the houses stood open to the night; nothing stirred; moonlight and silence lay over all. The night lay about him like a cloak. The air, soft and cool, caressed his cheek like the touch of a great furry paw. He gained confidence and began to walk quickly, though still keeping to the shadowed side. Nowhere could he discover the faintest sign of the great unholy exodus he knew had just taken place. The moon sailed high over all in a sky cloudless and serene.

Hardly realizing where he was going, he crossed the open market-place and so came to the ramparts, whence he knew a pathway descended to the high road and along which he could make good his escape to one of the other little towns that lay to the northward, and so to the railway.

But first he paused and gazed out over the scene at his feet where the great plain lay like a silver map of some dream country. The still beauty of it entered his heart, increasing his sense of bewilderment and unreality. No air stirred, the leaves of the plane trees stood motionless, the near details were defined with the sharpness of day against dark shadows, and in the distance the fields and woods melted away into haze and shimmering mistiness.

But the breath caught in his throat and he stood stockstill as though transfixed when his gaze passed from the horizon and fell upon the near prospect in the depth of the valley at his feet. The whole lower slopes of the hill, that lay hid from the brightness of the moon, were aglow, and through the glare he saw countless moving forms, shifting thick and fast between the openings of the trees; while overhead, like leaves driven by the wind, he discerned flying shapes that hovered darkly one moment against the sky and

71

then settled down with cries and weird singing through the branches into the region that was aflame.

Spellbound, he stood and stared for a time that he could not measure. And then, moved by one of the terrible impulses that seemed to control the whole adventure, he climbed swiftly upon the top of the broad coping, and balanced a moment where the valley gaped at his feet. But in that very instant, as he stood hovering, a sudden movement among the shadows of the houses caught his eye, and he turned to see the outline of a large animal dart swiftly across the open space behind him, and land with a flying leap upon the top of the wall a little lower down. It ran like the wind to his feet and then rose up beside him upon the ramparts. A shiver seemed to run through the moonlight, and his sight trembled for a second. His heart pulsed fearfully. Ilsé stood beside him, peering into his face.

Some dark substance, he saw, stained the girl's face and skin, shining in the moonlight as she stretched her hands towards him; she was dressed in wretched tattered garments that yet became her mightily; rue and vervain twined about her temples; her eyes glittered with unholy light. He only just controlled the wild impulse to take her in his arms and leap with her from their giddy perch into the valley below.

"See!" she cried, pointing with an arm on which the rags fluttered in the rising wind towards the forest aglow in the distance. "See where they await us! The woods are alive! Already the Great Ones are there, and the dance will soon begin! The salve is here! Anoint yourself and come!"

Though a moment before the sky was clear and cloudless, yet even while she spoke the face of the moon grew dark and the wind began to toss in the crests of the plane trees at his feet. Stray gusts brought the sounds of hoarse singing and crying from the lower slopes of the hill, and the pungent odor he had already noticed about the courtyard of the inn rose about him in the air.

"Transform, transform!" she cried again, her voice rising like a song. "Rub well your skin before you fly. Come! Come with me to

72

the Sabbath, to the madness of its furious delight, to the sweet abandonment of its evil worship! See! the Great Ones are there, and the terrible Sacraments prepared. The Throne is occupied. Anoint and come! Anoint and come!"

She grew to the height of a tree beside him, leaping upon the wall with flaming eyes and hair strewn upon the night. He too began to change swiftly. Her hands touched the skin of his face and neck, streaking him with the burning salve that sent the old magic into his blood with the power before which fades all that is good.

A wild roar came up to his ears from the heart of the wood, and the girl, when she heard it, leaped upon the wall in the frenzy of her wicked joy.

"Satan is there!" she screamed, rushing upon him and striving to draw him with her to the edge of the wall. "Satan has come. The Sacraments call us! Come, with your dear apostate soul, and we will worship and dance till the moon dies and the world is forgotten!"

Just saving himself from the dreadful plunge, Vezin struggled to release himself from her grasp, while the passion tore at his reins and all but mastered him. He shrieked aloud, not knowing what he said, and then he shrieked again. It was the old impulses, the old awful habits instinctively finding voice; for though it seemed to him that he merely shrieked nonsense, the words he uttered really had meaning in them, and were intelligible. It was the ancient call. And it was heard below. It was answered.

The wind whistled at the skirts of his coat as the air round him darkened with many flying forms crowding upwards out of the valley. The crying of hoarse voices smote upon his ears, coming closer. Strokes of wind buffeted him, tearing him this way and that along the crumbling top of the stone wall; and Ilsé clung to him with her long shining arms, smooth and bare, holding him fast about the neck. But not Ilsé alone, for a dozen of them surrounded him, dropping out of the air. The pungent odour of the anointed bodies stifled him, exciting him to the old madness of the Sabbath, the dance of the witches and sorcerers doing honour to the personified Evil of the world.

"Anoint and away! Anoint and away!" they cried in wild chorus about him. "To the Dance that never dies! To the sweet and fearful fantasy of evil!"

Another moment and he would have yielded and gone, for his will turned soft and the flood of passionate memory all but overwhelmed him, when—so can a small thing after the whole course of an adventure—he caught his foot upon a loose stone in the edge of the wall, and then fell with a sudden crash on to the ground below. But he fell towards the houses, in the open space of dust and cobblestones, and fortunately not into the gaping depth of the valley on the farther side.

And they, too, came in a tumbling heap about him, like flies upon a piece of food, but as they fell he was released for a moment from the power of their touch, and in that brief instant of freedom there flashed into his mind the sudden intuition that saved him. Before he could regain his feet he saw them scrabbling awkwardly back upon the wall, as though bat-like they could only fly by dropping from a height, and had no hold upon him in the open. Then, seeing them perched there in a row like cats upon a roof, all dark and singularly shapeless, their eyes like lamps, the sudden memory came back to him of Ilsé's terror at the sight of fire.

Quick as a flash he found his matches and lit the dead leaves that lay under the wall.

Dry and withered, they caught fire at once, and the wind carried the flame in a long line down the length of the wall, licking upwards as it ran; and with shrieks and wailings, the crowded row of forms upon the top melted away into the air on the other side, and were gone with a great rush and whirring of their bodies down into the heart of the haunted valley, leaving Vezin breathless and shaken in the middle of the deserted ground.

"Ilsé!" he called feebly; "Ilsé!" for his heart ached to think that she was really gone to the great Dance without him, and that he had lost the opportunity of its fearful joy. Yet at the same time his relief was so great, and he was so dazed and troubled in mind with the whole thing, that he hardly knew what he was saying, and only cried aloud in the fierce storm of his emotion....

The fire under the wall ran its course, and the moonlight came out again, soft and clear, from its temporary eclipse. With one last shuddering look at the ruined ramparts, and a feeling of horrid wonder for the haunted valley beyond, where the shapes still crowded and flew, he turned his face towards the town and slowly made his way in the direction of the hotel.

And as he went, a great wailing of cries, and a sound of howling, followed him from the gleaming forest below, growing fainter and fainter with the bursts of wind as he disappeared between the houses.

Part VI

"It may seem rather abrupt to you, this sudden tame ending," said Arthur Vezin, glancing with flushed face and timid eyes at Dr. Silence sitting there with his notebook, "but the fact is—er—from that moment my memory seems to have failed rather. I have no distinct recollection of how I got home or what precisely I did.

"It appears I never went back to the inn at all. I only dimly recollect racing down a long white road in the moonlight, past woods and villages, still and deserted, and then the dawn came up, and I saw the towers of a biggish town and so came to a station.

"But, long before that, I remember pausing somewhere on the road and looking back to where the hill-town of my adventure stood up in the moonlight, and thinking how exactly like a great monstrous cat it lay there upon the plain, its huge front paws lying down the two main streets, and the twin and broken towers of the cathedral marking its torn ears against the sky. That picture stays in my mind with the utmost vividness to this day.

"Another thing remains in my mind from that escape—namely, the sudden sharp reminder that I had not paid my bill, and the decision I made, standing there on the dusty highroad, that the small baggage I had left behind would more than settle for my indebtedness.

"For the rest, I can only tell you that I got coffee and bread at a café on the outskirts of this town I had come to, and soon after found my way to the station and caught a train later in the day. That same evening I reached London."

"And how long altogether," asked John Silence quietly, "do you think you stayed in the town of the adventure?"

Vezin looked up sheepishly.

"I was coming to that," he resumed, with apologetic wrigglings of his body. "In London I found that I was a whole week out in my reckoning of time. I had stayed over a week in the town, and it ought to have been September 15th,—instead of which it was only September 10th!"

"So that, in reality, you had only stayed a night or two in the inn?" queried the doctor.

Vezin hesitated before replying. He shuffled upon the mat.

"I must have gained time somewhere," he said at length—"somewhere or somehow. I certainly had a week to my credit. I can't explain it. I can only give you the fact."

"And this happened to you last year, since when you have never been back to the place?"

"Last autumn, yes," murmured Vezin; "and I have never dared to go back. I think I never want to."

"And, tell me," asked Dr. Silence at length, when he saw that the little man had evidently come to the end of his words and had nothing more to say, "had you ever read up the subject of the old witchcraft practices during the Middle Ages, or been at all interested in the subject?"

"Never!" declared Vezin emphatically. "I had never given a thought to such matters so far as I know—"

"Or to the question of reincarnation, perhaps?"

"Never—before my adventure; but I have since," he replied significantly.

There was, however, something still on the man's mind that he wished to relieve himself of by confession, yet could only with difficulty bring himself to mention; and it was only after the sympathetic tactfulness of the doctor had provided numerous openings that he at length availed himself of one of them, and stammered that he would like to show him the marks he still had on his neck where, he said, the girl had touched him with her anointed hands.

He took off his collar after infinite fumbling hesitation, and lowered his shirt a little for the doctor to see. And there, on the surface of the skin, lay a faint reddish line across the shoulder and extending a little way down the back towards the spine. It certainly indicated exactly the position an arm might have taken in the act of embracing. And on the other side of the neck, slightly higher up, was a similar mark, though not quite so clearly defined.

"That was where she held me that night on the ramparts," he whispered, a strange light coming and going in his eyes.

-oOo-

It was some weeks later when I again found occasion to consult John Silence concerning another extraordinary case that had come under my notice, and we fell to discussing Vezin's story. Since hearing it, the doctor had made investigations on his own account, and one of his secretaries had discovered that Vezin's ancestors had actually lived for generations in the very town where the adventure came to him. Two of them, both women, had been tried and convicted as witches, and had been burned alive at the stake. Moreover, it had not been difficult to prove that the very inn where Vezin stayed was built about 1700 upon the spot where the funeral pyres stood and the executions took place. The town was a sort of headquarters for all the sorcerers and witches of the entire region, and after conviction they were burnt there literally by scores.

"It seems strange," continued the doctor, "that Vezin should have remained ignorant of all this; but, on the other hand, it was not the kind of history that successive generations would have been anxious to keep alive, or to repeat to their children. Therefore I am inclined to think he still knows nothing about it.

"The whole adventure seems to have been a very vivid revival of the memories of an earlier life, caused by coming directly into contact with the living forces still intense enough to hang about the place, and, by a most singular chance, too, with the very souls who had taken part with him in the events of that particular life. For the mother and daughter who impressed him so strangely must have been leading actors, with himself, in the scenes and practices of witchcraft which at that period dominated the imaginations of the whole country.

"One has only to read the histories of the times to know that these witches claimed the power of transforming themselves into various animals, both for the purposes of disguise and also to convey themselves swiftly to the scenes of their imaginary orgies. Lycanthropy, or the power to change themselves into wolves, was everywhere believed in, and the ability to transform themselves into cats by rubbing their bodies with a special salve or ointment provided by Satan himself, found equal credence. The witchcraft trials abound in evidences of such universal beliefs."

Dr. Silence quoted chapter and verse from many writers on the subject, and showed how every detail of Vezin's adventure had a basis in the practices of those dark days.

"But that the entire affair took place subjectively in the man's own consciousness, I have no doubt," he went on, in reply to my questions; "for my secretary who has been to the town to investigate, discovered his signature in the visitors' book, and proved by it that he had arrived on September 8th, and left suddenly without paying his bill. He left two days later, and they still were in possession of his dirty brown bag and some tourist clothes. I paid a few francs in settlement of his debt, and have sent his luggage on to him. The daughter was absent from home, but the proprietress, a large woman very much as he described her, told my secretary that he had seemed a very strange, absent-minded kind of gentleman, and after his disappearance she had feared for a long time that he had met with a violent end in the neighboring forest where he used to roam about alone.

"I should like to have obtained a personal interview with the daughter so as to ascertain how much was subjective and how much actually took place with her as Vezin told it. For her dread of fire and the sight of burning must, of course, have been the intuitive memory of her former painful death at the stake, and have thus explained why he fancied more than once that he saw her through smoke and flame."

"And that mark on his skin, for instance?" I inquired.

"Merely the marks produced by hysterical brooding," he replied, "like the stigmata of the *religieuses*, and the bruises which appear on the bodies of hypnotized subjects who have been told to expect them. This is very common and easily explained. Only it seems curious that these marks should have remained so long in Vezin's case. Usually they disappear quickly."

"Obviously he is still thinking about it all, brooding, and living it all over again," I ventured.

"Probably. And this makes me fear that the end of his trouble is not yet. We shall hear of him again. It is a case, alas! I can do little to alleviate."

Dr. Silence spoke gravely and with sadness in his voice.

"And what do you make of the Frenchman in the train?" I asked further—"the man who warned him against the place, *à cause du sommeil et à cause des chats*? Surely a very singular incident?"

"A very singular incident indeed," he made answer slowly, "and one I can only explain on the basis of a highly improbable coincidence—"

"Namely?"

"That the man was one who had himself stayed in the town and undergone there a similar experience. I should like to find this man and ask him. But the crystal is useless here, for I have no slightest clue to go upon, and I can only conclude that some singular psychic affinity, some force still active in his being out of the same past life, drew him thus to the personality of Vezin, and enabled him to fear what might happen to him, and thus to warn him as he did.

"Yes," he presently continued, half talking to himself, "I suspect in this case that Vezin was swept into the vortex of forces arising out of the intense activities of a past life, and that he lived over again a scene in which he had often played a leading part, centuries before. For strong actions set up forces that are so slow to exhaust themselves, they may be said in a sense never to die. In this case they were not vital enough to render the illusion complete, so that the little man found himself caught in a very distressing confusion of the present and the past; yet he was sufficiently sensitive to recognize that it was true, and to fight against the degradation of returning, even in memory, to a former and lower state of development.

"Ah yes!" he continued, crossing the floor to gaze at the darkening sky, and seemingly quite oblivious of my presence, "subliminal up-rushes of memory like this can be exceedingly painful, and sometimes exceedingly dangerous. I only trust that this gentle soul may soon escape from this obsession of a passionate and tempestuous past. But I doubt it, I doubt it."

His voice was hushed with sadness as he spoke, and when he turned back into the room again there was an expression of profound yearning upon his face, the yearning of a soul whose desire to help is sometimes greater than his power.

Liber Tzaddi:
Book 90

by Aleister Crowley

In the name of the Lord of Initiation, Amen.

I fly and I alight as an hawk: of mother-of-emerald are my mighty-sweeping wings.

I swoop down upon the black earth; and it gladdens into green at my coming.

Children of Earth! rejoice! rejoice exceedingly; for your salvation is at hand.

The end of sorrow is come; I will ravish you away into mine unutterable joy.

I will kiss you, and bring you to the bridal: I will spread a feast before you in the house of happiness.

I am not come to rebuke you, or to enslave you.

I bid you not turn from your voluptuous ways, from your idleness, from your follies.

But I bring you joy to your pleasure, peace to your languor, wisdom to your folly.

All that ye do is right, if so be that ye enjoy it.

I am come against sorrow, against weariness, against them that seek to enslave you.

I pour you lustral wine, that giveth you delight both at the sunset and the dawn.

Come with me, and I will give you all that is desirable upon the earth.

Because I give you that of which Earth and its joys are but as shadows.

They flee away, but my joy abideth even unto the end.

I have hidden myself beneath a mask: I am a black and terrible God.

With courage conquering fear shall ye approach me: ye shall lay down your heads upon mine altar, expecting the sweep of the sword.

But the first kiss of love shall be radiant on your lips; and all my darkness and terror shall turn to light and joy.

Only those who fear shall fail. Those who have bent their backs to the yoke of slavery until they can no longer stand upright; them will I despise.

But you who have defied the law; you who have conquered by subtlety or force; you will I take unto me, even I will take you unto me.

I ask you to sacrifice nothing at mine altar; I am the God who giveth all.

Light, Life, Love; Force, Fantasy, Fire; these do I bring you: mine hands are full of these.

There is joy in the setting-out; there is joy in the journey; there is joy in the goal.

Only if ye are sorrowful, or weary, or angry, or discomforted; then ye may know that ye have lost the golden thread, the thread wherewith I guide you to the heart of the groves of Eleusis.

My disciples are proud and beautiful; they are strong and swift; they rule their way like mighty conquerors.

The weak, the timid, the imperfect, the cowardly, the poor, the tearful --- these are mine enemies, and I am come to destroy them.

This also is compassion: an end to the sickness of earth. A rooting-out of the weeds: a watering of the flowers.

O my children, ye are more beautiful than the flowers: ye must not fade in your season.

I love you; I would sprinkle you with the divine dew of immortality.

This immortality is no vain hope beyond the grave: I offer you the certain consciousness of bliss.

I offer it at once, on earth; before an hour hath struck upon the bell, ye shall be with Me in the Abodes that are beyond Decay.

Also I give you power earthly and joy earthly; wealth, and health, and length of days. Adoration and love shall cling to your feet, and twine around your heart.

Only your mouths shall drink of a delicious wine --- the wine of Iacchus; they shall reach ever to the heavenly kiss of the Beautiful God.

I reveal unto you a great mystery. Ye stand between the abyss of height and the abyss of depth.

In either awaits you a Companion; and that Companion is Yourself.

Ye can have no other Companion.

Many have arisen, being wise. They have said "Seek out the glittering Image in the place ever golden, and unite yourselves with It."

Many have arisen, being foolish. They have said, "Stoop down unto the darkly splendid world, and be wedded to that Blind Creature of the Slime."

I who am beyond Wisdom and Folly, arise and say unto you: achieve both weddings! Unite yourselves with both!

Beware, beware, I say, lest ye seek after the one and lose the other!

My adepts stand upright; their head above the heavens, their feet below the hells.

But since one is naturally attracted to the Angel, another to the Demon, let the first strengthen the lower link, the last attach more firmly to the higher.

Thus shall equilibrium become perfect. I will aid my disciples; as fast as they acquire this balanced power and joy so faster will I push them.

They shall in their turn speak from this Invisible Throne; their words shall illumine the worlds.

They shall be masters of majesty and might; they shall be beautiful and joyous; they shall be clothed with victory and splendour; they shall stand upon the firm foundation; the kingdom shall be theirs; yea, the kingdom shall be theirs.

In the name of the Lord of Initiation. Amen.

The Priest of Ra

by Manly P. Hall

What words are there in modern language to describe the great temple of Ammon Ra? It now stands amidst the sands of Egypt a pile of broken ruins, but in the heyday of its glory it rose a forest of plumed pillars holding up roofs of solid sandstone, carved by hands long laid to rest into friezes of lotus blossoms and papyrus and colored lifelike by pigments the secrets of which were lost with the civilization that discovered them. A checkerboard floor of black and white blocks stretched out until it was lost among the wilderness of pillars. From the massive walls the impassive faces of gods unnamed looked down upon the silent files of priests who kept alight the altar fires, whose feeble glow alone alighted the massive chambers throughout the darkness of an Egyptian night. It was a weird, impressive scene, and the flickering lights sent strange, ghostly forms scurrying among the piles of granite which rose like mighty altars from the darkness below to be lost in the shadows above.

Suddenly a figure emerged from the shadows, carrying in his hand a small oil lamp which pierced the darkness like some distant star, bringing into strange relief the figure of him who bore it. He appeared to be old, for his long beard and braided hair were quite gray, but his large black eyes shone with a fire seldom seen even in youth. He was robed from head to foot in blue and gold, and around his forehead was coiled a snake of precious metal, set with jeweled eyes that gave out flashes of light. Never had the light of Ra's chamber shone on a grander head or a form more powerful than that of the high priest of the temple. He was the mouthpiece of the gods and the sacred wisdom of ancient Egypt was impressed in fiery letters upon his soul. As he crossed the great room - in one hand the scepter of the priestcraft, in the other the tiny lamp - he was more like a spirit visitor from beyond the environs of death than a physical being, for his jeweled sandals made no sound and the sheen from his robes formed a halo of light around his stately form.

Down through the silent passageways, lined with their massive pillars, passed the phantom figure - down steps lined with kneeling sphinxes and through avenues of crouching lions the priest picked his way until at last he reached a vaulted chamber whose marble floor bore strange designs traced in some language long forgotten. Each angle of the many-sided and dimly-lighted room was filled by a seated figure carved in stone, so massive that its head and shoulders were lost in shadows no eye could pierce.

In the center of this mystic chamber stood a great chest of some black stone carved with serpents and strange winged dragons. The lid was a solid slab, weighing hundreds of pounds, without handle of any kind and the chest apparently had no means of being opened without the aid of some herculean power.

The high priest leaned over and from the lamp he carried lighted the fire upon an altar that stood near, sending the shadows of that weird chamber scurrying into the most distant corners. As the flame rose, it was reflected from the great stone faces above, which seemed to stare at the black coffer in the center of the room with their strange, sightless eyes.

Raising his serpent-wound staff and facing the chest of somber marble, the priest called out in a voice that echoed and re-echoed from every nook and cranny of the ancient temple:

"Aradamas, come forth!"

Then a strange thing happened. The heavy slab that formed the cover of the great coffer slowly raised as though lifted by unseen hands and there emerged from its dark recesses a slim, white-clad figure with his forearms crossed on his breast-the figure of a man perhaps thirty years old, his long, black hair hanging down upon his white-robed shoulders in strange contrast to the seamless garment that he wore. His face, devoid of emotion, was as handsome and serene as the great face of Ammon Ra himself that gazed down upon the scene. Silently Aradamas stepped from the ancient tomb and advanced slowly toward the high priest. When about ten paces from the earthly representative of the gods, he paused, unfolded his arms, and extended them across his chest in salutation. In one hand he carried a cross with a ring as the upper arm and this he proffered to the priest. Aradamas stood in silence as the high priest, raising his scepter to one of the great stone figures, addressed an invocation to the Sun-God of the universe. This finished, he then addressed the youthful figure as follows:

"Aradamas, you seek to know the mystery of creation, you ask that the divine illumination of the Thrice-Greatest and the wisdom that for ages has been the one gift the gods would shower upon mankind, be entrusted to you. Little you understand of the thing you ask, but those who know have said that he who proves worthy may receive the truth. Therefore, stand you here today to prove your divine birthright to the teaching that you ask."

The priest pronounced these words slowly and solemnly and then pointed with his scepter to a great dim archway surmounted by a winged globe of gleaming gold.

"Before thee, up those steps and through those passageways, lies the path that leads to the eye of judgment and the feet of Ammon Ra. Go, and if thy heart be pure, as pure as the garment that thou wearest, and if thy motive be unselfish, thy feet shall not stumble and thy being shall be filled with light. But remember that Typhon and his hosts of death lurk in every shadow and that death is the result of failure."

Aradamas turned and again folded his arms over his breast in the sign of the cross. As he walked slowly through the somber arch, the shadows of the great Unknown closed over him who had dedicated his life to the search for the Eternal. The priest watched him until he was lost to sight among the massive pillars beyond the silent span that divided the living from the dead. Then slowly falling on his knees before the gigantic statue of Ra and raising his eyes to the shadows that through the long night concealed the face of the Sun-God, he prayed that the youth might pass from the darkness of the temple pillars to the light he sought.

It seemed that for a second a glow played around the face of the enormous statue and a strange hush of peace filled the ancient temple. The high priest sensed this, for rising, he relighted his lamp and walked slowly away. His beacon of light shone fainter and fainter in the distance, and finally was lost to view among the papyrus blooms of the temple pillars. All that remained were the dying flames on the altar, which sent strange flickering glows over the great stone coffer and the twelve judges of the Egyptian dead.

In the meantime, Aradamas, his hands still crossed on his breast, walked slowly onward and upward until the last ray from the burning altar fire was lost to view among the shadows far behind. Through years of purification he had prepared himself for the great ordeal, and with a purified body and a balanced mind, he wended his way in and out among the pillars that loomed about him. As he walked along, there seemed to radiate from his being a faint golden glow which illuminated the pillars as he passed them. He seemed a ghostly form amid a grove of ancient trees.

Suddenly the pillars widened out to form another vaulted room, dimly lit by a reddish haze. As Aradamas proceeded, there appeared around him swirling wisps of this scarlet light. First they appeared as swiftly moving clouds, but slowly they took form, and strange misty figures in flowing draperies hovered in the air and held out long swaying arms to stay his progress. Wraiths of ruddy mist hovered about him and whispered soft words into his ears, while weird music, like the voice of the storm and the cries of night birds, resounded through the lofty halls. Still Aradamas walked on calm and masterful, his fine, spiritual face outlined by his raven locks in strange contrast to the sinuous forms that gathered around and tried to lure him from his purpose. Unmindful of strange forms that beckoned from ghostly archways and the pleading of soft voices, he passed steadily on his way with but one thought in his mind:

"Fiat Lux!" (Let there be light.)

The ghastly music grew louder and louder, terminating at last in a mighty roar. The very walls shook; the dancing forms swayed like flickering candle shadows and, still pleading and beckoning, vanished among the pillars of the temple.

As the temple walls tottered, Aradamas paused; then with slow measured step he resumed his search for some ray of light, finding always darkness deeper than before. Suddenly before him loomed another doorway, flanked on either side by an obelisk of carved marble, one black and the other white. Through the doorway glowed a dim light, concealed by a gossamer veil of blue silk.

As Aradamas slowly climbed the flight of steps leading to the doorway, there materialized upon the ground at his feet a swirl of lurid mist. In the faint glow that it cast, it twisted like some oily gas, filling the entire chamber with a loathsome miasma. Then out of this cloud issued a gigantic form - half human, half reptile. In its bloodshot eyes burned ruddy pods of demon fire, while great claw-like hands reached out to enfold and crush the slender figure that confronted it. Aradamas wavered for a single instant as the horrible apparition lunged forward, its size doubly magnified in the iridescent fog. Then the white-robed neophyte again slowly advanced, his arms still crossed on his breast. He raised his fine face, illumined by a divine light, and courageously faced the hideous specter. As he confronted the menacing form, for an instant it loomed over him like a towering demon. Suddenly Aradamas raised the cross he carried and held it up before the monster. As he did so, the Crux Ansata gleamed with a wondrous golden light, which, striking the oily, scaly monster, seemed to dissolve its every particle into golden sparks. As the last of the demon guardians vanished before the rays of the cross, a bolt of lightning flashed through the ancient hallways and, striking the veil that hung between the obelisks, rent it down the center and disclosed a vaulted chamber with a circular dome, dimly lighted by invisible lamps.

Bearing his now flaming cross, Aradamas entered the room and instinctively gazed upward to the lofty dome. There, floating in space, far above his head, he saw a great closed eye surrounded by fleecy clouds and rainbow colors. Long Aradamas gazed upon the wonderful sight, for he knew that it was the Eye of Horus, the All-Seeing Eye of the gods.

As he stood there, he prayed that the will of the gods might be made known unto him and that in some way he might be found worthy to open that closed eye in the temple of the living God.

As he stood there gazing upward, the eyelid flickered. As the great orb slowly opened, the chamber was filled with a dazzling, blinding light that seemed to consume the very stones with fire. Aradamas staggered. It seemed as if every atom of his being was scorched by the effulgence of that glow. He instinctively closed his eyes and now he feared to open them, for in that terrific blaze of splendor it seemed that only blindness would follow his action. Little by little, a strange feeling of peace and calm descended upon him and at length he dared to open his eyes to find that the glare was gone, the entire chamber was bathed in a soft, wondrous glow from the mighty Eye in the ceiling. The white robe he had worn had also given place to one of living fire which blazed as though with the reflection of thousands of lesser eyes from the divine orb above. As his eyes became accustomed to the glow, he saw that he was no longer alone. He was surrounded by twelve white-robed figures who, bowing before him, held up strange insignia wrought from living gold.

As Aradamas looked, all the figures pointed, and as he followed the direction of their hands, he saw a staircase of living light that led far up into the dome and passed the Eye in the ceiling.

With one voice, the twelve said: "Yonder lies the way of liberation."

Without a moment's hesitation, Aradamas mounted the staircase, and with feet that seemed to barely touch the steps, climbed upward into the dawn of a great unknown. At last, after climbing many steps, he reached a doorway that opened as he neared it. The breath of morning air fanned his cheek and a golden ray of sunshine played among the waves of his dark hair. He stood on the top of a mighty pyramid, before him a blazing altar. In the distance, far over the horizon, the rolling sands of the Egyptian desert reflected the first rays of the morning sun which, like a globe of golden fire, rose again out of the eternal East. As Aradamus stood there, a voice that seemed to issue from the very heavens chanted a strange song, and a hand, reaching out as it were from the globe of day itself, placed a serpent wrought of gold upon the brow of the new initiate.

"Behold Khepera, the rising sun! For as he brings the mighty globe of day out of the darkness of night, between his claws, so for thee the Sun of Spirit has risen from the darkness of night and in the name of the living God, we hail thee Priest of Ra."

A Weird Tale

by William Q. Judge

Part I

The readers of this magazine have read in its pages, narratives far more curious and taxing to belief than the one I am about to give fragments of. The extraordinary Russian tale of the adept at the rich man's castle when the infant assumed the appearance of an old man will not be forgotten. But the present tale, while not in the writer's opinion containing anything extremely new, differs from many others in that I shall relate some things, I myself saw. At this time too, the relation is not inopportune, and perhaps some things here set down may become, for many, explanations of various curious occurrences during the past five years in India and Europe.

To begin with, this partial story is written in accordance with a direction received from a source which I cannot disobey and in that alone must possess interest, because we are led to speculate why it is needed now.

Nearly all of my friends in India and Europe are aware that I have travelled often to the northern part of the South American continent and also to Mexico. That fact has been indeed noticed in this magazine. One very warm day in July 1881, I was standing at the vestibule of the Church of St. Theresa in the City of Caracas, Venezuela. This town was settled by the Spaniards who invaded Peru and Mexico and contains a Spanish-speaking people. A great crowd of people were at the door and just then a procession emerged with a small boy running ahead and clapping a loud clapper to frighten away the devil. As I noticed this, a voice in English said to me "curious that they have preserved that singular ancient custom." Turning I saw a remarkable looking old man who smiled peculiarly and said, "Come with me and have a talk." I complied and he soon led me to a house which I had often noticed, over the door being a curious old Spanish tablet devoting the place to the patronage of St. Joseph and Mary. On his invitation I entered and at once saw that here was not an ordinary Caracas house. Instead of Venezuelan servants, there were only Hindus such as I had often seen in the neighboring English Island of Trinidad; in the place of the disagreeable fumes of garlic and other things usual in the town, there hung in the air the delightful perfumes known only to the Easterners. So I at once concluded that I had come across a delightful adventure.

Seating ourselves in a room hung with tapestry and cooled by waving punkahs that evidently had not been long put up, we engaged in conversation. I tried to find out who this man was, but he evaded me. Although he would not admit or deny knowledge of the Theosophical Society of Madame Blavatsky or of the Mahatmas, he constantly made such references that I was sure he knew all about them and had approached me at the church designedly. After quite a long talk during which I saw he was watching me and felt the influence of his eye, he said that he had liberty to explain a little as we had become sufficiently acquainted. It was not pleasure nor profit that called him there, but duty alone. I referred to the subterranean passages said to exist in Peru full of treasure and then he said the story was true and his presence there connected with it. Those passages extended up from Peru as far as Caracas where we then were. In Peru they were hidden and obstructed beyond man's power to get them but in this place the entrances were not as well guarded although in 1812 an awful earthquake had levelled much of the town. The Venezuelans were rapacious and these men in India who knew the secret had sent him there to prevent any one finding the entrances. At certain seasons only, there were possibilities of discovery; the seasons over, he could depart in security, as until the period came again no one could find the openings without the help and consent of the adepts. Just then a curious bell sound broke on the air and he begged me to remain until he returned as he was called, and then left the room. I waited a long time filled with speculations, and as it was getting late and past dinner hour I was about to leave. Just as I did so a Hindu servant quickly entered and stood in front of the only door. As he stood there I heard a voice say as if through a long pipe: "Stir not yet." Reseating myself, I saw that on the wall, where I had not before noticed it, hung a curious broad silver plate brightly shining. The hour of the day had come when the sun's light struck this plate and I saw that on it were figures which I could not decipher. Accidentally looking at the opposite wall, I saw that the plate threw a reflection there upon a surface evidently prepared for that purpose and there was reproduced the whole surface of the plate. It was a diagram with compass, sign and curious marks. I went closer to examine, but just at that moment the sun dipped behind the houses and the figures were lost. All I could make out was that the letters looked like exaggerated Tamil or Telugu — perhaps Zend. Another faint bell sounded and the old man returned. He apologized, saying he had been far away, but that we would meet again. I asked where, and he said, "In London." Promising to return I hurried away. Next day I could not find him at all and discovered that there were two houses devoted to Joseph and Mary and I could not tell which I had seen him in. But in each I found Spaniards, Spanish servants and Spanish smells.

In 1884 I went to London and had forgotten the adventure. One day I strolled into an old alley to examine the old Roman wall in the Strand which is said to be 2,000 years old. As I entered and gazed at the work, I perceived a man of foreign aspect there who looked at me as I entered. I felt as if he knew me or that I had met him, but was utterly unable to be sure. His eyes did not seem to belong to his body and his appearance was at once startling and attractive. He spoke to the attendant, but his voice did not help me. Then the attendant went out and he approaching me, said:

"Have you forgotten the house of Joseph and Mary?"

In a moment I knew the expression that looked out through those windows of the soul, but still this was not the same man. Determined to give him no satisfaction I simply said, "no," and

97

waited.

"Did you succeed in making out the reflection from the silver plate on the wall?" Here was complete identification of place, but not of person.

"Well," I said, "I saw your eyes in Caracas but not 'your body,' He then laughed and said, "I forgot that, I am the same man, but I have borrowed this body for the present and must indeed use it for some time, but I find it pretty hard work to control it. It is not quite to my liking. The expression of my eyes of course you knew, but I lost sight of the fact that you looked at the body with ordinary eyes."

Once more I accompanied him to his residence and when not thinking of his person but only listening with the soul, I forgot the change. Yet it was ever present, and he kindly gave me an account of some things connected with himself, of absorbing interest. He began in this way.

"I was allowing myself to deceive myself, forgetting the *Bhagavad Gita* where it tells us, that a man is his soul's friend and his soul's enemy, in that retreat in Northern India where I had spent many years. But the chance again arose to retrieve the loss incurred by that and I was given the choice of assuming this body."

At this point again, I heard the signal bell and he again left me. When he returned, he resumed the story.

If I can soon again get the opportunity, I will describe that scene, but for the present must here take a halt.

Part II

There are many who cannot believe that I have been prevented from writing the whole of this tale at once, and they have smiled when they read that I would continue it "if allowed." But all who know me well will feel that there is some truth in my statement. It may interest those who can read between the lines to know that I attempted several times to finish the tale so as to send it all in one batch to the magazine, but always found that at the point where the first chapter ends my eyes would blur, or the notes ready for the work became simply nonsense, or some other difficulty intervened, so that I was never until now able to get any further with it than the last instalment. It is quite evident to me that it will not be finished, although I know quite well what it is that I have to say. This part must, therefore, be the last, as in trying to reach a conclusion much time is wasted in fighting against whatever it is that desires to prevent my going into full details. In order then to be able to get out even so much as this I am compelled to omit many incidents which would perhaps be interesting to several persons; but I shall try to remember particularly and relate what things of a philosophical nature were repeated to me.

As I sat there waiting for the host to come back, I felt the moral influence of another mind, like a cool breeze blowing from a mountain. It was the mind of one who had arrived at least at that point where he desired no other thing than that which Karma may bring, and, even as that influence crept over me, I began to hear a voice speaking as it were through a pipe the end of which was in my head, but which stretched an immense distance into space making the voice sound faint and far off. It said:

"The man whose passions enter his heart as waters run into the unswelling passive ocean obtaineth happiness; not he who lusteth in his lusts. The man who having abandoned the lusts of the flesh worketh without inordinate desires, unassuming, and free from pride, obtaineth happiness. This is divine dependence. A man being possessed of this confidence in the Supreme goeth not astray: even at the hour of death should he attain it he shall mix with the incorporeal nature of Brahm. He who enjoyeth the *Amreeta* that is left of his offerings obtaineth the eternal spirit of Brahm the Supreme."

The atmosphere of the room seemed to give the memory great retentive power, and when on returning to my room that night I fell upon those sentences in the *Bhagavad Gita*. I knew that they had come to me from a place or a person for whom I should have respect.

Occupied with such thoughts, I did not notice that my host had returned, and looking up was somewhat startled to see him sitting at the other side of the apartment reading a book. The English clothes were gone and a white Indian dhoti covered him, and I could see that he wore round his body the Brahmanical cord. For some reason or other he had hanging from a chain around his neck an ornament which, if it was not Rosicrucian, was certainly ancient.

Then I noticed another change. There seemed to have come in with him, though not by the door, other visitors which were not human. At first I could not see them, though I was aware of their presence, and after a few moments I knew that whatever they were they rushed hither and thither about the room as if without purpose. They had yet no form. This absorbed me again so that I said nothing and my host was also silent. In a few more moments these rushing visitors had taken from the atmosphere enough material to enable them to become partly visible. Now and then they made a ripple in the air as if they disturbed the medium in which they moved about, just as the fin of a fish troubles the surface of the water. I began to think of the elemental shapes we read of in Bulwer Lytton's *Zanoni*, and which have been illustrated in Henry Kunrath's curious book on the *Cabala of the Hebrews*.

"Well," said my strange friend, "do you see them? You need have no fear, as they are harmless. They do not see you, excepting one that appears to know you. I was called out so as to try if it were possible for you to see them, and am glad that you do."

"And the one that knows me," said I. "Can you identify it in any way?"

"Well," said he, "let us call it *he*. He seems to have seen you — been impressed with your image just as a photograph is on a plate — somewhere or other, and I also see that he is connected with you by a name. Yes, it is . . . ."

And then he mentioned the name of an alleged elemental or nature spirit which at one time, some years ago, was heard of in New York.

"He is looking at you now, and seems to be seeking something. What did you have or make once that he knew of?"

I then recollected a certain picture, a copy of an Egyptian papyrus of the Hall of Two Truths showing the *trial of the Dead*, and so replied, regretting that I had not got it with me to show my friend. But even as I said that, I saw the very picture lying upon the table. Where it came from I do not know, as I had no recollection of bringing it with me. However, I asked no questions, and waited, as my host was looking intently at the space above my head.

"Ah, that is what he was looking for, and he seems to be quite pleased," he said, as if I could hear and see just as he did. I knew he referred to the elemental.

In another moment my attention was rivetted on the picture. Its surface bobbed up and down as if waves ran over it, and crackling sounds rose from every part. They grew louder and the motion ceased, while from a certain point arose a thin whitish vapor that wavered unsteadily to and fro. Meanwhile the strange visitors I have mentioned seemed to rush about more in the vicinity of the paper, while now and again one of them took what looked like a flying leap from one end of the room to the other, with a queer faint boom of a metallic character following his rapid motion.

Part III

Here I must draw the veil unwillingly. Let me violate the unities and the frame of this tale by just putting down a few sentences, leaving it to the imagination to draw inferences.

"Those strange delineations of form? Quite easily. They were seen by the seeresses in the temple, It is quite true that elementals have no form as such . . . But there are undoubtedly types, and those Egyptians were not the men to do anything unscientifically . . . There is an occult reason why, although without form, these particular shapes were assumed. And having been once assumed and seen thus by the seer, they always repeated that form to those persons. So, the representative of the astral light or of wisdom or the recording angel, is yellow in color, very tall, with a long bill like a stork. Or the one who takes the weight of the soul is always seen with a jackal's head. . . . No, there is no prohibition against telling the occult reason. It is merely this: were it told, only one in a thousand hearers would see any meaning or reason in it. . . . Let your mind reflect also upon the peculiarity that all the judges sitting above there have heads alike, while in color they differ, each one having a feather, the emblem of truth, on his head . . . No, it is not Hindu, and yet it is the same. They used to say, and I think you may find it in one of their books, that 'everything is in the Supreme soul, and the Supreme soul in everything.' So, the great truth is one, while it can be seen in a thousand different ways. We Egyptians took a certain view and made every symbol consistent and of a class consonant with our view. . . . And just as the Hindus are accused of being idolaters because they have represented Krishna with eight arms standing on the great elephant, we, who did not picture an eight-armed divinity, are charged with having worshipped jackals, cats and birds . . .

"Yes, it is a pity, but the sand that buries Egypt has not been able to smother the great voice of that sphinx, the *esoteric doctrine*. But not through us except in some such manner as this, now and then.

In India the light burns, and in a living-people still resides the key — ."

Just then the bobbing of the picture began again and the same whitish column wavered over it. The faint boom of the airy elementals recommenced, and again claimed my attention, and then the picture was still.

I may say that the whole of the conversation has not been given. It is not necessary that it should be. My host had maintained perfect silence all the while, and seemed to await my voice, so I said:

"What could have induced you to leave those peaceful places where true progress may be gained."

"Well," he replied, "very likely they were peaceful, and quite truly progress was possible, but you do not appreciate the dangers also. You have read *Zanoni*, and perhaps have an exaggerated idea of the horrible Dweller of the Threshold, making of her a real person or thing. But the reality is much worse. When you get into what you have called the 'peaceful places,' this power becomes tenfold stronger than it is found to be on the plane in which we now live in London."

"Why? I had supposed that there, free from the cankering anxieties of modern life, the neophyte sailed happily on through plain seas to the shores of the fortunate isles."

"Far from that. On that plane it is found that, although from the spiritual sun there falls upon us the benign influence of those great sages who, entering para-nirvana, throw off their accumulated goodness for our benefit, the evil influence that is focused by the dark side of the moon falls as well, and with its power undiminished. The little temptations and difficulties of your life are as nothing compared to that struggle for then it is realized that the self is the enemy of the self, as well as its friend."

"But," said I, "was the fault committed a great one, that it should condemn you to this task?"

"No, not great as you term it. But quite great enough; and in consequence I had to take my choice. In Caracas you saw me as an illusion of a certain character. There I did what was required, the illusion being perfect except as to the eyes. Now you see another illusion, and yet at the same time a reality such as is connoted by that word when used by modern scientists. It is a body that lives and will die. The Karma is hard perhaps, but I grumble not. But is it not an illusion in every sense when you know that although this body speaks and thinks, still, I the speaker am not visible to you?"

These words are not mine. If some of them seem meaningless or queer to many readers, do not blame the writer. There are those who can understand. There are yet others who have latent thoughts that need but these words to call them into life. I cannot give any greater detail than the above as to himself, because he had reasons for preventing me, although he might perhaps, himself tell more to another.

One curious thing of interest he said, which will furnish some with food for thought. It was when I referred to the use of the body he had, so to say, *borrowed*, that he said:

"Don't you know that many experiments are possible in that way, and that some students are taught peculiarly? I have stood aside from this earthly tabernacle many a time to let in those who, notwithstanding that they operated the machine well enough and made quite a respectable use of it, did not know what they did. They were, if you like, dreaming. While here, in this body, they were essentially it, for the time speaking its words, thinking its thoughts and not able to control it. Not desiring to in fact, because they were completely identified with it. When they waked up in their own apartments either a singular dream whispered a fragmentary song through their brain, or they retained no remembrances; whatever of it. In such a case the body, being really master, might do or say that which I would not — or the occupier, temporarily strong, might say out of real recollection things having relation only to that life of which his hearers would have no knowledge."

Just then some clock struck. The atmosphere seemed to clear itself. A strange and yet not unfamiliar perfume floated through the room, and my host said, "Yes, I will show you a verse someone tells me to show you."

He walked over to the table, took up a queer little book printed in Sanskrit, yellow with age and seeming to have been much used. Opening it he read:

"This supreme spirit and incorruptible Being, even when it is in the body, neither acteth, nor is it affected, because its nature is without beginning and without quality. As the all-moving Akas, or ether, from the minuteness of its parts, passeth everywhere unaffected, even so the Omnipresent spirit remaineth in the body unaffected. As a single sun illumines the whole world, even so doth the spirit enlighten ever body. They who, with the eye of wisdom, perceive the body and the spirit to be thus distinct, and that there is a final release from the animal nature, go to the Supreme."

And just like that, I never saw him again.

Strange Story of a Red Jar

by Arthur Machen

If you ever chance to spend a few weeks in the County of Monmouth, and are one of those clever people who know where to look for what is good, you will not fail to roam over the hills and across the valleys till you come to a little town called Uske. This town lies beside the fair river of the same name, and is sheltered on every side by wooded hills and sweet, greeny slopes; and to the east you can see the enchanted forest of Wentwood, where there are deep dells, shady alleys, rocks with water everlastingly dripping from them, and the finest black cherries that anybody could wish to taste. But, if you once cross the bridge and get into Uske, you will have plenty to look at without thinking of Wentwood, that is, if you are fond of quaint houses, wild old-fashioned gardens, and odd nooks and corners of every sort. And, better than all, there are old tales and legends still lingering about the sunny streets, and sleeping on the settles next to the fire; but it is getting rather difficult to wake them up now, because you see they are very old. They are, in fact, the last vestiges of the good old monks, who had a Priory in Uske, and this tale I am going to tell is considered by experienced judges to be as pleasant a story as any of them, because it has such a fine moral, without which a story is no more use than a wasp without his sting.

You must know, then, that there was once a monk at the Priory, named Brother Drogo, who was regarded by everybody as a splendid specimen of a monk; and not without reason, for he stood six feet high, and had a waist like a wine-tub. He had roving twinkling black eyes, a firm mouth, and a voice like the roar of the pedal-pipes of the organ, and it must be confessed that in his quire habit he looked a well-proportioned man, and a pillar of the Church. As for his intellect, all the brethren allowed him to be an admirable logician, an orthodox divine, and the best judge of sauces, seasonings, hot relishes, sweetmeats, and preserved dainties of the whole convent, and this was saying a great deal. It was Brother Drogo's science and deep knowledge of the nature of things, and of how to mingle hot and sweet together, that made the pious brethren long for Lent and fast-days, and desire to mortify their throats with curious dishes, of which none but himself and the cook ever understood the composition. But yet this was not Brother Drogo's greatest art; for he was the cellarer of the Priory, and took care of the casks in the cellar, and of that pleasant vineyard on a southern slope, where the sun was nearly always to be found; and, if he were great in the kitchen and the larder, he was far greater in the affairs of the fragrant world below. But here his one fault got the better of him, and sometimes played him queer tricks; for, to tell the truth, Brother Drogo used now and then to get very drunk. When in this state he usually saw visions, which made some esteem him a very holy man (since it is only such that are blessed in this fashion); but others said that his visions were of the wrong sort and should be kept out of the monastic Chronicle. However this may be the last vision that he ever saw was such a wonderful one that it lasted him the rest of his life, since he never touched anything but water afterwards; and this was the manner of it.

It was a very hot drowsy sort of day in the beginning of September; a day when the sickles were busy in the corn-fields round Uske, a day of blue dim mists over the woods and hills and the river, a day of mellowed golden sunlight good for the vines and apples and pears and plums, and all the autumn fruits that were ripening in those tangled gardens of Gwent. In the castle above the town the lords and ladies were lying in the shade upon the grass and listening to the ballads and love-songs of the minstrel Master Jehan de Laune of Paris town; and the girls let the squires and pages tickle them and snatch sly kisses as much as ever they liked;

because it was too hot to scream and they knew it was right to bear and forbear. In the Priory the monks were (most of them) asleep and dreaming holy dreams that made them smile as they slept; but Brother Drogo was wide awake and walking up and down the cloister. Why was this? Well it was because he was terribly thirsty, and felt as if a Lollard were being roasted somewhere at the back of his throat, and the reason that he did not drink was that he had doubts whether he should ever stop if he once began. This was in fact a knotty case of conscience and it puzzled the good man and made him feel thirstier than ever, which was natural since theology is known to be a dry and thirsty science. It is bad enough when two or three divines are muddling a question between them, but this unfortunate monk had to be Praeses, Opponent, and Respondent all at once; and he found that it was necessary for him to take a little wine to clear his brain, for being a conscientious man he wished to settle this point before doing anything else. He therefore picked his way past a dozen or so of monks, all smiling very hard, and went along a dark passage, and began to go down the steps to the cellar. Now the steps were many and by reason of their great age, uneven; so it was slow work getting to the bottom, and the Cellarer had to stop short very often and tap his skull, for the cool air from below seemed to make his blood hotter than before. And when he stopped he held up his lamp and looked at the walls, which had been decorated in rather a curious manner by an ancient monk who had been dead a good many hundred years. This artist's fancy had led him to suppose that views of Purgatory and warmer places would be a nice ornament to the cellar stair; but whether he intended all these flames, fagots, and streams of fire as a sort of whet for the wine, or whether he meant to say "that's what'll come to you if you get drunk" is more than I can tell. But these pictures made Brother Drogo feel warmer and warmer, though he couldn't help looking at them; and in one place where a fine powerful demon was sousing a big monk in a cauldron of fire and poking him with a three-pronged fork to see if he were done, the Cellarer was forced to discern a huge resemblance between the monk's features and his own. However he trod the last step in due time, and stood in the vaulted cellar, the which had aisles, transepts, side chapels, and ambulatories in abundance, but there were casks everywhere of all shapes and sizes, and a few curious-looking jars with Greek letters cut on them. In this shadowy world of wine Brother Drogo stood awhile and gazed about in an abstracted kind of way, rolling his tongue in his mouth and telling his tale on his fingers as he thought of Burgundy, Beaulne, Champagne, and all the vintages of the fair land of France, of Valdepenas and Amontillado, of the juice of the Rhine mountains, and of the famous wines of Italy, which are drawn from the very mouth of the fire below. But the Cellarer's thirst was such a stupendous one that he could not see his way to allaying it on any of these; so he just drew himself a pint of his own red wine of Uske, and sat down on a stone form to consider things. When he had finished his draught he began to walk about among the casks and to peer into odd shelves and crannies in out of the way recesses and blind corners of the cellar, muttering to himself all the time "Burgundy, Beaulne, Champagne, Valdepenas, Amontillado, Montepulciano" as if he were bidding the beads of St. Bacchus. By chance he came to a nook in the darkest part of the cellar, in the which nothing was kept, nor had been for many a long day; and holding up his lamp and peering about the dim and shadowy wall he saw faintly a great red jar, of the most ancient and uncouth form imaginable, graved all over with ivy leaves, vine tendrils, pine cones and a pomp of nymphs and fauns dancing all around it. But there was no mark, nor label to say what this jar held; so Brother Drogo found it was his duty as Cellarer to look a little more closely into the matter. Indeed he had his doubts as to whether this jar was a good Christian, so he got on a stone step and began to use his tools on the jar's mouth, which was covered tightly with black pitch. And as he cut this pitch away faint odors of delicious fragrance began to steal out tickling Brother Drogo's weakest places. "The Prior will thank me for this day's work" thought he; and thus he cut the last piece away and the soul of the jar poured its whole fragrance out upon him like a breeze from the Islands in the High Levant, and went past into the cellar, and up the stair into the cloister where the monks were asleep, and out into the town so that the townsfolk said to one another, "'Tis a balmy day, indeed marvelously balmy." As for the girls in the castle their gallants squeezed them a little more closely, and they smiled and seemed to think everything was being properly performed and going on nicely; but then it was a sweet gale that blew upon them.

But Brother Drogo said to himself "one cup—one little cup—of this wonderful wine will quite quench my thirst; better than a hogshead of any other wine; indeed if I were now half-seas-over, it would be my duty to taste it; am I not Cellarer? How shall I bring the matter before the Prior without having tasted?" You see Brother Drogo had not read Aristotle for nothing, so he gently inclined the jar to his cup, and let a dark purple stream run slowly like oil into it, till it was quite full. And when he tasted he had drained the cup, and when he had drained the cup, he knew that he, the Cellarer of the Convent of St. Mary, was a sinful man that had gloried all his days in a nice discrimination of various juices, when in point of fact, he had that moment tasted wine for the first time in his life. But instead of running up the stairs and telling the Prior, Brother Drogo drank and drank again, cup after cup, till he got chimes in his ears, fire in his veins, and a mizmaze in his brain. This veracious history does not say how many cups Brother Drogo lifted out of the red jar; but it was certainly a great many for he was a man of large capabilities. However as he was drawing down the jar to fill once more that little cup, he seemed suddenly to fall asleep, and to have down cushions laid under his head, but this strange circumstance happened so suddenly that he had no time to take notes; and it is not possible to give so full a description of the affair as I should have wished. But the really strange part of the tale is that when he had slept till he could sleep no more, and woke up again, he was no longer in the cellar of the Convent at Uske; how this happened neither he nor I nor anybody else have ever made out, but it is certainly a fact that Brother Drogo rubbed his eyes and found himself lying on green grass. And when he had rubbed his eyes a second time, had stood up and looked about him, he saw that he was standing on the highest point of a mountain girt around with woods of dark pine-trees, and dwarf oak thickets, and brakes of tangled undergrowth. Below very far was a city of a strange fashion, and beyond the city mountains rising one above the other; and behind him was the sea of a very deep blue. Before the Cellarer had finished wondering where he was and how he got there, his ears caught a noise of jangling and clashing of brass on brass, with shrill flute notes, beating of drums, and loud cries and hails now from one quarter and now from another, gathering together and drawing towards him. I do not see what Brother Drogo could do but open his mouth; it is certain that he did so, for he could not recollect what passage it was that led out of the cellar to the top of this mountain. But while he was thinking the matter over, the drums, tambourines, cymbals, single flutes, double flutes, and loud calling grew loud enough to deafen one; and all at once he was surrounded on all sides by a company of girls whose clothes seemed to be at the wash, for there was not enough of linen (or of anything else) to make a kerchief on the whole company. And when they began to dance round the poor man, calling to him in a tongue he did not understand, he began to be afraid he had got into bad company, not suited for a monk of St. Bennet's rule. But he could not help allowing that these girls had very nice figures and seemed to be able to make a great noise. "If I were a layman," thought he, "it would be different, but these amusements are not quite proper for ecclesiastical persons." Round, around they whirled in dancing and the din of cymbals clashed louder yet; but then the figures of the naked girls became shadows and their music was hushed to a dull murmur. The next thing Brother Drogo heard was the words of the Prior of his Convent, saying "He will yet live, and drink another cup." "Of water only" answered the poor Cellarer, who began to think he was always to be moving, from cellar to mountain and from mountain to his bed. In fact, he had been found, after much seeking, lying on his back in the cellar, with a nasty cut on his head, a great wine jar lying in shards beside him, and a pool of dark red wine on the floor giving forth a fragrance that made the monks sniff eagerly. Some persons have said that Brother Drogo must have slipped backwards, knocking his skull against the edge of a stone ascent, and pulling the wine jar after him. These persons make out that he dreamt whatever he saw, but I am disposed to think them rather too clever for this dull world of ours. But as I said at the beginning of the tale the Cellarer kept to water for the rest of his life, and leaving the cellar to another hand became the chief gardener of the Priory, and grew such worts, and flowers, and fruits as were not to be seen elsewhere in all Gwent. Indeed he invented that great green plum, as big as an egg, that melts in the mouth as sweet as honey, and is rightly called "Soif de Dru," or " Drogo's Thirst."

And the moral of this history is—Leave old jars on the shelf. It seems to me a good one.

Psychic Tendencies and Development

by H. W. Percival

Epidemics of different kinds appear in every age. Many epidemics have visited us, among them psychic epidemics. A psychic epidemic prevails when many people in a community give rein to that side of man's nature which inclines to the mysterious and they deal with such subjects as omens, fortune telling, dreams, visions, communication with creatures of the invisible worlds, and the communication with and worship of the dead. These epidemics, like other movements, come in cycles or waves. When they are well underway there appears a general tendency among people to develop as sport or as study psychism and psychology. Different peoples, different conditions of climate, environment and the particular cycle or period of time bring out different phases of psychism.

Owing to the modern materialistic turn of the scientific mind, the study of psychology, the science of the soul, has been discredited and any suggestions as to the possession, development or inclination to the study of psychic faculties have been disposed of by the scientific mind with ridicule and contempt. If one was in possession of psychic faculties, or believed in their development, he was considered by the hard thinkers to be either an impostor, a hypocrite, or to be mentally unbalanced or a fool. And some of the keenest thinkers who gladly would have investigated psychism and psychology have not been strong enough to stand against the weapons of ridicule and contempt, as used by their fellows.

But the cycle has turned. The scientific mind has with great seriousness begun to investigate the psychic faculties in man. It is now the fashion for people to be psychic: to see, smell and hear strange things, and to feel creepy and spooky. This is a quick reaction from modern materialism, but primarily it is due to the season, the cycle or period of time which we have entered. This cycle is causing the physical organism of man to become more susceptible to the influences from the invisible worlds which surround and permeate our physical world, although these worlds are as they were before the organism of man was so responsive to them.

For ages past the human mind has been intent on ideals and objects which have been material in their nature; but since the latter part of the nineteenth century the mind has been directed to new lines of thought, to new ideals and aspirations. It has been pointed out that there are worlds hitherto undreamed of which may be opened up to man. It has been shown there are possibilities for his development far beyond anything which he had considered himself capable of attempting or attaining.

As a result of such thoughts, many societies have been formed for the study and research into psychical matters. Some of these societies teach and encourage the development of psychic faculties. Some make a business of it, and some prey on the credulity of people by pretending to have and to impart for money powers and knowledge which they have not.

But psychic tendencies are not restricted to societies specially organized for that study and practice. The psychic wave has affected religious bodies as it has those not particularly interested in religion. In fact, religion has always depended on the psychic nature and tendencies of man for its strength and power over his mind. Following the first teachings of any founder of a religion and his associates there have been developed hard and fast rules and observances, which are imposed on the people. The advocates of the particular religion have often departed from its true teaching to gain followers, to build up a church and to increase the power of the church. To do this they abandoned reason and appealed to the psychic emotional nature of man. They first stirred up his psychic nature and inflamed his sympathies, then controlled and enslaved his mind. It is more difficult to control man by an intellectual process. The mind can never be enslaved by an appeal to reason. A religion always controls man by inflaming his emotional psychic nature.

When any spiritual movement is started there is usually the tendency of its followers to degenerate by psychic practices. If such practices are indulged in before members of that body are qualified physically, morally and mentally to begin the practices, disruption and confusion and other unfortunate happenings will inevitably result. It may be well to say a few words concerning the advent of psychical tendencies and spiritual aspirations now manifest.

The psychic wave now passing over the world began in the latter part of the last century. In a section of one of the New England States there had been a spiritistic outbreak which then seemed to be a local affair. But spiritism is only one of the phases of psychic tendencies. The psychic tendencies were really inaugurated in New York by Madam Blavatsky, who formed the Theosophical Society, in 1875. The Theosophical Society was formed by Madame Blavatsky as a working instrument through which Theosophy was to be given to the world. The Theosophical Society was of course composed of men and women of the age, whereas Theosophy is the wisdom of the ages. Through the Theosophical Society were presented by Madam Blavatsky certain theosophical teachings. These teachings apply to subjects covering the entire range of thought and introduced to the Western world problems not before considered. They apply to mundane affairs as well as to ideal and spiritual aspirations and attainments. However enigmatical an individual Madam Blavatsky may have appeared to some people, the teachings which she brought are worthy the most serious consideration and thought.

The many societies now engaged in psychical matters, and the mental and spiritual development of man, have received their real impulse through the Theosophical Society. The Theosophical Society made it possible for representatives of other races and religions to come to the Western world and present their different doctrines to the people. Western people who would not have tolerated or given ear to religions other than their own were, owing to the strange Theosophical teachings, interested and made ready to consider anything from "the heathen." Eastern races came, they found a hearing in the West. Whether it is to be to the advantage of the West will depend on the integrity of the Eastern teachers, honesty in the presentation of their doctrines, and on purity of life.

Following the passing of Madam Blavatsky, the Theosophical Society was for a time convulsed and thrown into confusion by that which Madam Blavatsky had advised against: division and separation. Even then, although the Society was divided against itself, the teachings were the same. But as time progresses, some of the teachings are slightly changed. With continued division, there has also been a departure from the philosophical and spiritual tone of the teachings and a tendency to psychic practices. The Theosophical Society cannot be an exception to the law: if its members continue to give way to their psychic tendencies, they, as have other similar bodies in the past, will degenerate morally, mentally and physically and end in ignominy and reproach. There is one other possibility: if some inimical being of power should get control of one of the now existing Theosophical Societies, he might by force of his will use the philosophical teachings with such changes as might suit his convenience, and, dominating that body, build up a church or powerful hierarchy. Such a course would be most unfortunate for humanity as the being of power, through the hierarchy, would have a hold on and dominate and enslave the human mind even more than the religions of the past or present have done. The Theosophical Society has done a great work in giving a portion of Theosophy to the world, but it would be much better to have every one of its societies stamped out of existence than to have all or any part of it become such a curse to humanity as to establish a so-called spiritual hierarchy from among its members with all the human weaknesses and shortcomings.

In other civilizations, those, for instance, of Greece, Egypt, and India, psychics have been made use of by the priests. Their psychics were used as oracles, for purposes of divination, of discovery, in the treatment of diseases and for communication with the invisible powers. The psychics of our civilization have been used for similar purposes, but more especially have they been used for the curiosity seekers, to produce sensation, and to gratify the inordinate desires of test hunters and wonder lovers.

But the psychic tendency in our civilization, if turned in the right direction and controlled, will assist us in building up a civilization greater and grander and nobler than any of the past. On the other hand, psychic tendencies may hasten our destruction and bring our history to a close by insane desire for money, by the love of luxury, or by sensual gratification and worship of the dead. This civilization should be greater than others because of the physical organisms of the people, their adaptability to conditions, their ability to change conditions, their inventiveness, their readiness to grasp and make the best of a situation, their being equal to emergencies, and on account of their nervous force and mental activity.

There are disadvantages, as well as benefits, which may result from psychic tendencies and their development. Whether we shall have benefit instead of harm from psychic tendencies depends on the individual as it does on the nation. The influences which affect the psychic come from the visible and invisible worlds. Through our visible world there are constantly playing and interacting the forces and powers of the invisible worlds. Each world, visible or invisible, has its races and beings, peculiar to itself. The entities from the invisible worlds come in contact with man through his psychic nature, and, according to his psychic tendencies, the invisible influences and entities will act on him and stimulate him to action. Creatures and powers at present undreamed of, act on man through his emotional psychic nature. His mental visions and imaginary sounds and strange feelings are often caused by the presence of these forces and beings. While man is partitioned off from them by his limited physical sight, and walled in and protected from them by a strong, healthy physical body, he is safe, for his physical body is to him as a fortress. But should the walls of the fortress be weakened, as it may by foolish practices, then inimical creatures of the invisible worlds will break through and make a captive of him. The elemental powers of nature will drive him to all manner of excesses and he will be unable to resist any of their attacks. They will sap him of his vitality, make him incapable of controlling his physical body, enslave him to his desires, obsess his body, and dishonor and lower him below the level of a beast.

In the present stage of the ordinary man's development, psychic tendencies are as useless to him as whisky and astronomical instruments to an American Indian. The benefit of psychic tendencies and psychic faculties are that they make man responsive to nature, and put him in sympathy with his fellow man. They are the instruments which he may use for seeing into and understanding the details of nature and of all natural phenomena. The psychic nature, if properly trained, will enable man to more readily change and improve his physical body and to bring it under control. The psychic nature, when controlled and cultured, will enable man to bring into the physical world the treasures which he may gather from the invisible worlds, to bring into physical life all the desirable ideals and ideal forms stored up in the world of thought, the mental world, and to make the physical world ready for the knowledge from the spiritual world.

The tendency of those interested in psychics and psychic development is to abandon reason or make their reasoning faculties subservient to the new psychic faculties and worlds opening up to them. This abandonment of reason at once unfits them for progress. To make faculties which are new, useful, their uses must be understood and care applied, until the new faculties are known and brought under the control of the reasoning being. Reason should never be abandoned.

People of the Western world, particularly in the United States, will continue to develop psychic tendencies, but they should appreciate and have a better understanding of the uses and abuses of psychic tendencies and their development, instead of as at present allowing their psychic nature to manifest and run riot.

Under present conditions, a normal healthy man is one whose physical cell-body is closely knit with his astral molecule-body, the design principle of form on which the physical tissue of the body is built.

The general make-up and characteristics of a psychic are usually quite different from those of a normal healthy man. A psychic is one whose astral molecule-body of form is loosely knit with the physical cell-body of cells, and the astral form, on account of its loose connection with the physical cell tissue, is more susceptible to the influences of the worlds around it which correspond to its nature.

There are natural-born psychics and psychics who become such by development. Psychics are born as such, owing to the physiological and psychic condition of their parents or the general conditions prevailing before and at the time of birth. All with psychic tendencies should become acquainted with the philosophy concerning the psychic nature before attempting psychic practices. The best means of combatting the dangers of psychism is the study of philosophy and the living of a clean life.

Those not born psychics may develop a psychic organism and become psychics by giving up their will and becoming negative and giving way to all influences which they feel, or by a weakening and breaking down of the resisting powers of the animal body through a vegetarian diet. These are the irresponsible psychics. But psychic organisms might also be developed by directing one's actions according to reason, by the control of one's appetites and desires, by the performance of one's duties, or by development of the mind through control of its functions. If the latter course is followed, the psychic faculties will develop as naturally as a tree puts forth leaves, buds, blossoms and fruit in the proper seasons. These are the trained psychics. There are very few.

The make-up of a psychic is like that of a kaleidoscope. The physical body is like the casing or sheath, the many-sided facets within like the senses in use; the colored and colorless objects which fall about on the glass at every turn of the case like the thoughts and desires which are thrown and reflected on the glass or astral body, the eye through which the pattern is seen is like the mind in the body, and the intelligence which discriminates concerning what is seen is like the real man. As kaleidoscopes differ, so do psychics differ in their quality and as individuals who handle the kaleidoscope differ, so do those who make use of their psychic nature.

The terms "psychic," "psychism" and "psychology" are frequently used, but the distinctions are not as sharply drawn as they should be. The word psychic comes from the Greek word Psyche, a beautiful mortal maiden, the human soul, who underwent many trials and hardships, but at last became an immortal by uniting in marriage with Eros. Psyche itself means the soul, and all words with this prefix have to do with the soul; thus psychism is that which is of the soul. But psychism as used today has more to do with the nervous physiological action of the personality than with the soul proper. Psychology is soul science, or science of the soul.

In a more particular sense, however, and according to the Greek myth, Psyche in man is the astral molecule-body, or design principle of form. Psyche was said to be mortal because the astral molecular body of form lasts only as long as does the physical body, its counterpart. The father, too, of Psyche was a mortal because as the past personality he also was subject to death. The astral molecular body of form of the present life is the sum total and result of one's thoughts in the preceding life -in the same sense that in the present life one's desires and thoughts are building for his next life the astral molecular form body, on and according to which his physical matter will be molded. Psyche is beloved by Eros, which name is used in different senses. The Eros who first loves Psyche is the principle of desire which, unseen by Psyche, unites with her. Psyche the astral molecular body of form is the body through which all sensations are experienced as the pleasures and pains of the senses; is the giver of pleasure to desire. But as the mortal form, it dies. If, however, Psyche, the astral molecular body of form, the mortal soul, can successfully go through all of the hardships and trials imposed upon it, it passes through a metamorphosis similar to that of Psyche and her symbol, the butterfly, and is transformed into a being of a different order: from the mortal into an immortal. This takes place when the astral molecular body of form is changed from the temporary mortal into a permanent immortal; it is then no longer subject to death, for it has grown out of the larval state of the physical body of flesh. Eros is sometimes used to designate that portion of the higher mind, of the individuality, which enters into the astral molecular body of form and is incarnate in the physical body. It is owing to the love of the mind for its mortal form, Psyche, in the physical body, that Psyche, the personal human soul, is eventually saved, raised from the dead and made an immortal by union with the mind. The different uses made of the names Psyche and Eros and the mystery of the relation of Eros to Psyche, the mortal personal human soul, will be more clearly understood as one becomes acquainted with his own nature and learns to distinguish between and relate the different constituent parts and principles which make him the complex being which he is. A study of psychology will prove to man that he is made up of many Psyches, or souls.

There are four kinds of psychics: the physical psychic, astral psychic, mental psychic, and the spiritual psychic, as represented in the zodiac by the respective signs: Libra, Virgo-Scorpio, Leo-Sagittarius, Cancer-Capricorn. In the different zodiacs within the absolute zodiac, each zodiac represents man.

One may develop his physical psychic nature by breaking down his physical health, by improper food, by fasting, by ill treatment and abuse of the body, such as taking alcohol, and drugs, by inflicting pain, by austerities, by flagellation, or by excessive sexual indulgence.

The astral psychic nature may be developed by gazing fixedly at a bright spot, or by sitting alone in the dark in a passive condition of mind, or by pressing the eyeballs and following the colors seen, or by magnetic treatment, or by being hypnotized, or by the burning of certain incense, or by using a ouija board, or by attending spiritistic seances, or by the repetition and chanting of certain words, or by the assuming of physical postures, or by the exhaling, inhaling and retention of the breath.

The mental psychic nature, is to be developed by mental practices, such as the forming of mental pictures, by giving mental forms to mental colors, and by controlling all the functions of the mind through meditation.

The development of the spiritual psychic nature is brought about by the control of the functions of the mind when one is able to identify himself in the spiritual world of knowledge, in which all the other phases of the psychic nature are comprehended.

The attainment, powers or faculties developed by the foregoing classes of psychics are:

First: the belief in and practice of physical spiritual husbands and wives, or the intercourse held with actual incubi or succubi, or the obsession of one's body by some strange entity.

Second: the developing of clairvoyance or clairaudience, as a materialization medium, or a trance medium, or a precipitation medium, or somnambulism.

Third: the faculty of second-sight, or psychometry, or telepathy, or divination, or ecstasy, or a powerful imagination- the image-building faculty.

And finally, fourth: the attaining of knowledge, or the faculty of prophecy, or the power to create intelligently- the power to Will.

The House of the Past

by Algernon Blackwood

One night a Dream came to me and brought with her an old and rusty key. She led me across fields and sweet-smelling lanes, where the hedges were already whispering to one another in the dark of the spring, till we came to a huge, gaunt house with staring windows and lofty roof half hidden in the shadows of very early morning. I noticed that the blinds were of heavy black, and that the house seemed wrapped in absolute stillness.

"This," she whispered in my ear, "is the House of the Past. Come with me and we will go through some of its rooms and passages; but quickly, for I have not the key for long, and the night is very nearly over. Yet, perchance, you shall remember!"

The key made a dreadful noise as she turned it in the lock, and when the great door swung open into an empty hall and we went in, I heard sounds of whispering and weeping, and the rustling of clothes, as of people moving in their sleep and about to wake. Then, instantly, a spirit of intense sadness came over me, drenching me to the soul; my eyes began to burn and smart, and in my heart, I became aware of a strange sensation as of the uncoiling of something that had been asleep for ages. My whole being, unable to resist, at once surrendered itself to the spirit of deepest melancholy, and the pain of my heart, as the Things moved and woke, became in a moment of time too strong for words...

As we advanced, the faint voices and sobbings fled away before us into the interior of the House, and I became conscious that the air was full of hands held aloft, of swaying garments, of drooping tresses, and of eyes so sad and wistful that the tears, which were already brimming in my own, held back for wonder at the sight of such intolerable yearning.

"Do not allow this sadness to overwhelm you," whispered the Dream at my side. "It is not often They wake. They sleep for years and years and years. The chambers are all full, and unless visitors such as we come to disturb them, they will never wake of their own accord. But, when one stirs, the sleep of the others is troubled, and they too awake, till the motion is communicated from one room to another and thus finally throughout the whole House.... Then, sometimes, the sadness is too great to be borne, and the mind weakens. For this reason, Memory gives to them the sweetest and deepest sleep she has and she keeps this old key rusty from little use. But, listen now," she added, holding up her hand: "do you not hear all through the House that trembling of the air like the distant murmur of falling water? And do you not now... perhaps... remember?"

Even before she spoke, I had already caught faintly the beginning of a new sound; and, now, deep in the cellars beneath our feet, and from the upper regions of the great House as well, I heard the whispering, and the rustling and the inward stirring of the sleeping Shadows. It rose like a chord swept softly from the huge unseen strings stretched somewhere among the foundations of the House, and its tremblings ran gently through its walls and ceilings. And I knew that I heard the slow awakening of the Ghosts of the Past.

Ah, me, with what terrible inrushing of sadness I stood with brimming eyes and listened to the faint dead voices of the long ago.... For, indeed, the whole House was awakening; and there presently rose to my nostrils the subtle, penetrating perfume of age: of letters, long preserved, with ink faded and ribbons pale; of scented tresses, golden and brown, laid away, ah, how tenderly! among pressed flowers that still held the inmost delicacy of their forgotten fragrance; the scented presence of lost memories -- the intoxicating incense of the past. My eyes o'er-flowed, my heart tightened and expanded, as I yielded myself up without reserve to these old, old influences of sound and smell. These Ghosts of the Past -- forgotten in the tumult of more recent memories -- thronged round me, took my hands in theirs, and, ever whispering of what I had so long forgot, ever sighing, shaking from their hair and garments the ineffable odors of the dead ages, led me through the vast House, from room to room, from floor to floor.

And the Ghosts -- were not all equally clear to me. Some had indeed but the faintest life, and stirred me so little that they left only an indistinct, blurred impression in the air; while others gazed half reproachfully at me out of faded, colorless eyes, as if longing to recall themselves to my recollection; and then, seeing they were not recognized, floated back gently into the shadows of their room, to sleep again undisturbed till the Final Day, when I should not fail to know them.

"Many of these have slept so long," said the Dream beside me, "that they wake only with the greatest difficulty. Once awake, however, they know and remember you even though you fail to remember them. For it is the rule in this House of the Past that, unless you recall them distinctly, remember precisely when you knew them and with what particular causes in your past evolution they were associated, they cannot stay awake. Unless you remember them when your eyes meet, unless their look of recognition is returned by you, they are obliged to go back to their sleep, silent and sorrowful, their hands unpressed, their voices unheard, to sleep and dream, deathless and patient, till...."

At this moment, her words died away suddenly into the distance and I became conscious of an overpowering sensation of delight and happiness. Something had touched me on the lips, and a strong, sweet fire flashed down into my heart and sent the blood rushing tumultuously through my veins. My pulses beat wildly, my skin glowed, my eyes grew tender, and the terrible sadness of the place was instantly dispelled as if by magic. Turning with a cry of joy, that was at once swallowed up in the chorus of weeping and sighing round me, I looked... and instinctively stretched forth my arms in a rapture of happiness towards... towards a vision of a Face... hair, lips, eyes; a cloth of gold lay about the fair neck, and the old,

old perfume of the East - ye stars, how long ago – was in her breath. Her lips were again on mine; her hair over my eyes; her arms about my neck, and the love of her ancient soul pouring into mine out of eyes still starry and undimmed. Oh, the fierce tumult, the untold wonder, if I could only remember! .... That subtle, mist-dispelling odor of many ages ago, once so familiar... before the Hills of Atlantis were above the blue sea, or the sands had begun to form the bed of the Sphinx. Yet wait; it comes back; I begin to remember. Curtain upon curtain rises in my soul, and I can almost see beyond. But that hideous stretch of the years, awful and sinister, thousands upon thousands .... My heart shakes, and I am afraid. Another curtain rises and a new vista, farther than the others, comes into view, interminable, running to a point among thick mists. Lo, they too are moving, rising, lightening. At last, I shall see... already I begin to recall... the dusky skin... the Eastern grace, the wondrous eyes that held the knowledge of Buddha and the wisdom of Christ before these had even dreamed of attainment. As a dream within a dream, it steals over me again, taking compelling possession of my whole being... the slender form... the stars in that magical Eastern sky... the whispering winds among the palm trees... the murmur of the river's waves and the music of the reeds where they bend and sigh in the shallows on the golden sand. Thousands of years ago in some aeonian distance. It fades a little and begins to pass; then seems again to rise. Ah me, that smile of the shining teeth... those lace-veined lids. Oh, who will help me to recall, for it is to far away, too dim, and I cannot wholly remember; though my lips are still tingling, and my arms still outstretched, it again begins to fade. Already there is a look of sadness too deep for words, as she realizes that she is unrecognized... she, whose mere presence could once extinguish for me the entire universe... and she goes back slowly, mournfully, silently to her dim, tremendous sleep, to dream and dream of the day when I must remember her and she must come where she belongs...

She peers at me from the end of the room where the Shadows already cover her and win her back with outstretched arms to her age-long sleep in the House of the Past.

Trembling all over, with the strange odor still in my nostrils and the fire in my heart, I turned away and followed my Dream up a broad staircase into another part of the House.

As we entered the upper corridors, I heard the wind pass singing over the roof. Its music took possession of me until I felt as though my whole body were a single heart, aching, straining, throbbing as if it would break; and all because I heard the wind singing round the House of the Past.

"But, remember," whispered the Dream, answering my unspoken wonder, "that you are listening to the song it has sung for untold ages into untold myriad ears. It carries back so appallingly far; and in that simple dirge, profound in its terrible monotony, are the associations and recollections of the joys, grieves, and struggles of all your previous existence. The wind, like the sea, speaks to the inmost memory," she added, "and that is why its voice is one of such deep spiritual sadness. It is the song of things for ever incomplete, unfinished, unsatisfying."

As we passed through the vaulted rooms, I noticed that no one stirred. There was no actual sound, only a general impression of deep, collective breathing, like the heave of a muffled ocean. But the rooms, I knew at once, were full to the walls, crowded, rows upon rows .... And, from the floors below, rose ever the murmur of the weeping Shadows as they returned to their sleep, and settled down again in the silence, the darkness, and the dust. The dust .... Ah, the dust that floated in this House of the Past, so thick, so penetrating; so fine, it filled the throat and eyes without pain; so fragrant, it soothed the senses and stilled the heart; so soft, it parched the tongue, without offence; yet so silently falling, gathering, settling over everything, that the air held it like a fine mist and the sleeping Shadows wore it for their shrouds.

"And these are the oldest," said my Dream, "the longest asleep," pointing to the crowded rows of silent sleepers. "None here have wakened for ages too many to count; and even if they woke you would not know them. They are, like the others, all your own, but they are the memories of your earliest stages along the great Path of Evolution. Someday, though, they will awake, and you must know them, and answer their questions, for they cannot die till they have exhausted themselves again through you who gave them birth."

"Ah me," I thought, only half listening to or understanding these last words, "what mothers, fathers, brothers may then be asleep in this room; what faithful lovers, what true friends, what ancient enemies! And to think that someday they will step forth and confront me, and I shall meet their eyes again, claim them, know them, forgive, and be forgiven... the memories of all my Past...."

I turned to speak to the Dream at my side, but she was already fading into dimness, and, as I looked again, the whole House melted away into the flush of the eastern sky, and I heard the birds singing and saw the clouds overhead veiling the stars in the light of coming day.

The King of the Wood

by Aleister Crowley

Part I

He kept in the shadow of the grove. It was bright moonlight, but he did not walk there. He walked so that it was impossible to discover his object. Even in the murk of the grove one could see the great head thrust forward, and imagine the intensity of the eyes, as he paced restlessly among the trees. Apparently, then, he was seeking something. Yet he passed again and again over the same places. Once he came near to a pool of moonlight in the glade, near enough for a sudden flash to strike into the depth of the darkness; one could divine that in his hand was a drawn sword. The stealth and vigilance of his manner now gave the clue to his mind's one thought; he was on guard; he expected attack. But whence? No scene could be more mirrored peace.

The moon shone brightly on the hills to the north of the grove; to the south a declivity led to an embowered lake, set in the cup of an old crater, so deep that even the wanton winds of the hills rarely ventured to tease its silver with their breath, as maids may with a glass.

Part of this slope had been cut away, and a great terrace wall extended some two hundred yards or more; the water lay against its foot. Upon this terrace stood a small and silent temple adorned with Doric columns of peperino. The cornices were more elaborate, and carved of marble; there were also friezes of terra cotta, while under the moonlight the tiles of gilded bronze which roofed it returned her silver kiss with a ruddier glow.

This shrine was set in a great mass of woodland, absolutely still on that windless night, save where, bubbling from the basalt, a spring ran over the pebbles, and fell in a series of cascades into the lake. No other sound broke in upon the night, for the tread of the watcher was muted; it was spring; there were no fallen leaves, but moss and violets were soft and fragrant for his foot.

Presently the strange man gave a wild gesture, as of impatience. He stepped deliberately into the moonlight where a marble statue stood among the beeches and the oaks, to mark the place, perhaps, of some fallen monster of the forest. He raised his great head to the moon and shook his sword — was it in triumph or in agony? Muttering strange words. One could see the sweat upon his forehead as he lifted it to that clear light.

It was a marvelous head. Browning might have used it as a model for his John the Pannonian.

"Here's John the Smith's rough-hammered head. Great eye, gross jaw and griped lips do what granite can to give you the crown-grasper."

For every mark of the self-made man was stigmatized in him. The arms were long, the hands enormous, powerful and sinewy, knotted and calloused. The figure was gigantic in height, but lean and ill-proportioned; the back was bent as if from years of toil. The head itself was almost absurdly large; the jaw was thrust forward like a gorilla's, and the expression of the mouth was in keeping. The eyes expressed cunning and savagery as well as resolution and pride. This last quality was written all over the man.

His carriage was the incarnation of self-esteem; and yet — ? Yes, there was agony mingled with the triumph of his gesture. His eyes were tired with watching; fear had crept in to mar their brilliance.

Was it that a leaf rustled? In an instant the man leaped from the side of the statue, and was lost in the blackness of the wood.

A moment later, through a little avenue, came a woman running and gasping for breath. At every opening in the wood she stopped and cried aloud. Her fear, witnessed by loose tresses and disordered raiment, quivered in her voice; but it also lent her unnatural keenness of perception, for she saw the man with the sword when he was still many yards distant. Instantly she changed her course and dashed toward him, falling at his feet in an attitude of intense supplication. Her gasps repressed themselves enough for her to utter one loud cry, "Sanctuary, O King!"

The strange man answered "You are safe here; go on into the temple" in an even untroubled voice, as if the incident were common and formal. He seemed to redouble his vigilance. The woman rose to her feet, as if to obey his directions, then staggered and fell. "My strength is gone," she cried. "Lead me to the temple."

The King looked yet more intently towards a certain tree that stood by itself in the glade in an oval space of green-sward. It was an aged oak towering and massive. He thought he saw a movement in the trees that encircled it at a respectful distance, like courtiers about a king. For all answer to the woman, he cut her to the earth with a single sweep of his sword, and bounded forward.

The movement that he had seen turned instantly to frantic flight; but those long limbs had paced every alley of the wood by night and day for many a year; the fugitive had no chance of escape. Before he had gone twenty yards, the king was on him; a sword-thrust pierced him back to breast, and he fell headlong. The other never stooped; he was sure of his sword-work; he turned instantly on his heel and resumed his restless pacing.

Yet presently an idea seemed to strike him; he dragged the bodies into the open; and, drawing a piece of cord from his garment, swung them from a low branch of the great oak. He gave a low grim laugh; then settled himself at the foot of the tree; in a moment he was fast asleep.

Part II

Elsewhere there was another man on guard that night, but he took his duty less seriously. He was a short burly slave, immensely strong, with a round brutal head and thick bull neck, his hair so short and curled, and his complexion so dark, that one might have guessed an admixture of African blood. He leaned on the short Roman pilum with its broad blade and heavy shaft, and he was frankly bored with life. From time to time he sat down and rested on the steps of the villa which he guarded, and looked across toward the moon over the woods that lay below him. He could just see the lake and the temple upon the terrace above it, for the moon lit them to life, although they were some miles away. But he had no thought towards them but as scenery; he had no idea of the tragedy even then being enacted in those distant groves.

So dull was he that he lost all sense of his duty; he was awakened smartly by a light touch upon his shoulder. Before he could turn, a figure wrapped and muffled in a dark robe flitted past him from the house, and made toward the woods that sheltered it upon the west. He followed it with his eyes.

The figure turned, made a single gesture of beckoning, sped on to the shelter of the trees. The slave hesitated. He looked up at the villa; all was dark. I'll risk it, he thought, and moved swiftly toward the shadow where the mysterious one had now disappeared.

Before he had taken three paces within the darkness, he came up with it. A white hand came from the vesture, caught his and pressed it, led him some ten yards further where a statue of Pan stood in a circular basin in which a fountain played. Around the basin the ground was terraced, and thick grown with moss. The figure moved to the one spot where moonlight fell, and took a seat, drawing the slave down also. There was a moment's pause.

The slave seemed bewildered; the other evidently enjoyed the fact. Then, with a sudden movement, the white hand drew away the cloak from the face, and showed it. The mouth moved in three words: "I have thee."

But the slave groveled on the moss in an ecstasy of terror. He could only murmur "Lady! Lady!" again and again. "I am thy slave," he gasped out at last.

The face of the lady, that was even and rounded, with crisp ringlets set about it, and an expression of sternness and even harshness fixed on the thin firm curled lips of her long mouth as from strong habit, softened with laughter. "Am I not thine, rather?" she said softly, and, stooping down, caught the head of the slave in her arms, and began to eat it up with kisses. . . .

Suddenly she perceived that dawn was about to break. She disengaged herself, and went swiftly and silently to the house. On the steps she staggered twice.

The slave had slept. He woke in consternation to find the sun up, and he away from his post. He dashed back; there was nobody stirring. Discipline in that house was lax, now that the master had been away a month at the war. When he was at home, dawn saw every man at work; things were easier now.

The slave's mind went back to the events of the night; he cast his eyes to the distant temple. Diana save me! he cried; I have had a wondrous dream.

Part III

It was the first of many such dreams. Night after night, in one way or another, the lady of the villa pursued her fancy. As the summer grew on the woods, she seemed to wax in her infatuation, but the first leaves that fell were no warning to her. Rather she glanced at the fruits that ripened in the orchard, and took them for the omens of her perfected passion. There was only one hint of winter in her year, a rumor that news had come to Rome of a great battle in the North, and of the utter defeat of the barbarians.

Intrigue has many demerits, and is (besides) morally indefensible; but it has this advantage, that it makes men proud, and, so, ambitious. Many a career has begun with an infringement of the moral law. So, as the summer passed, the slave became unhappy in his happiness.

Till now he had been contented to be a slave; he had never considered the possibility of any escape from that condition; but now, although the Lady Clodia had managed to confer many a sly favor, he was ill content. Her very gifts only served to quicken the new-born spirit of freedom. But she never spoke of asking for his freedom when the master returned; he knew instinctively that she would not dare to do so; and the rigid social system of the Republic gave no hope of any issue from his strait by any efforts of his own.

One passionate night in September the lovers were again by the fountain of Pan where first they had given and taken all that heart would. The nightingales were silent, though, and the moon, far in her wane, was not yet in the East.

The slave was melancholy, and the quick insight of her strange love understood.

"I am the slave of a slave," she whispered in his ear, so low that the fountain flowed in her words like an accompaniment, "and I would be the slave of a king."

"You have made me a king," he answered, "I have all the passions of a king. I can hardly hold my hand when Caius orders me to do his bidding." "I am glad," she said simply. "I knew you were worthy. Listen: I am going to hurt you. I have had bad news. Letters came today from the army; my lord is on his way home after the victory; he will be here in two nights more. If you dare, you shall be a king!" The slave looked up in sudden horror. "Oh, no," she laughed, "we are not to play Aegisthus and Clytemnestra; if I ruled Rome it could be done, but not in times like these. No; but you shall be a king — the King of the Wood! and I shall be the most pious of all the votaries of Diana!" She said it lightly; but his eyes were fixed in fear and horror upon her .

The Roman look came fierce into her face. "You dare!" she cried, "for me you dare!" and with a single movement she threw an arm about his neck and fastened her mouth on his, while with the other hand she drew a sword from beneath her cloak, and put it in his hand. Tensely he gripped it, and returned her caress with fury. "I will do it," he cried; "may great Diana aid!" She tightened her clasp on him. "I am condemning you to death," she hissed, "I am your murderess. My mouth drinks up your blood. I love you." The slave was silent; he abandoned himself more fiercely than he had ever yet done to her caresses; they had sealed their guilty love by the one passion on earth that is mightier than that — the lust of blood!

Part IV

The next day the hue-and-cry was up; for the slave had run away. But in a day the news came back that search was useless; he had taken sanctuary with Diana at Nemi across the lake.

The Lady Clodia consoled her husband easily. "He was a worthless fellow, idle and impudent," she said; "he was not worth his keep. If he had not run off, I should have asked you to sell him."

But the slave only remained in sanctuary three days; in that time he learnt all that he wanted to know. He disappeared, and none knew whither.

He was in Rome itself. Clodia had furnished him with an ample purse, and with the disguise which had served him on his journey. He had taken lodgings with a shoemaker, representing himself as a sailor from Sicily. Here he led an austere life, refusing the temptations of Rome. He spent many hours every day with famous swordsmen, and trained his hands to war, and his fingers to fight. He kept his body in admirable condition by constant attendance at the gymnasia and the baths, and his soul by unwearying attendance at the temple of Diana.

The only thing that he neglected was his purse; and though Clodia had been royally liberal, it became clear to him at the feast of the Sun, which we now call Christmas, that he must take the giant step which led back to Clodia — or on to death.

Accordingly, on the very next day, he left Rome, and took his way across the Campagna to the Alban Hills. He was a very different man to the slave who had sat drowsing on the steps of the villa. Not only was he alert and active, every inch an athlete, but the months of love and of freedom had kindled his eye; he threw back his head as he marched, and sang aloud the war songs of the Romans.

Almost had he come to the first foot of the spur when he espied an old woman by the wayside. She asked him alms, and offered to tell his fortune. He remembered his poverty; then with a laugh bethought him that he would never need money again, and tossed his purse with its few golden coins to the beldam. She grasped it eagerly, amazed. "I see a wonderful fortune for you, my lad," she cried. "You are going to be a prosperous farmer; you will have love, you will have honor and fame and every blessing, for many a year. But beware of going to Nemi; if you go there, you will die there." With that, and confused benedictions from Jupiter and Diana and Mars and many another, she hobbled off.

An ill omen! thought the youth. But he kept sturdily on his way. Yet revolving it in his mind, now a thousand times more active than it had been in his slave-days, he suddenly saw a secret meaning to the oracle. He actually was going to be a farmer — of sorts; he meant to gather one of the fruits of earth. He must succeed, else love and honor could never come to him; and as for dying at Nemi, why, of course he would die there!

But not now! "It was Diana herself, who came to hail me!" With that he quickened his pace, and breasted joyously and confidently the slopes of the hills.

As night fell, he began to come to the neighborhood of the temple. His step became wary. Presently he came to a point long since marked down by him, where an avenue in the trees permitted a sight of the shrine, and of the pathway trodden by the dreadful king on that night of spring which saw the two corpses, fruit of the fatal oak. Here he buried the sword that Clodia had given him, for none but the king himself might bear arms in that sacred wood. He then crept a little — a very little — further along the avenue to where there was a mound of turf beneath a great beech. Here he hid himself, covering his body with fallen leaves, and waited.

It was a fearful night. Snow lay here and there upon the ground. The trees were somber and spectral, black and jagged against a lowering and stormy sky, and the rising wind made melancholy music in the branches, its own howl like a wolf's. It eddied in the hollows of the hills, and even stirred the icy waters of the lake that lurked in the black crater. The moon rose early; already she was high mid-heaven, as the watcher saw when the wind tore the clouds apart, and let her pallid witch-glamour fall on the staggering earth. As on that fatal night of spring, her ray fell also on the glint of steel. The king still kept his lonely vigil, still prowled in darkness and in terror of storm.

The hours passed with infinite stealth; the wind now loosed its fury from the Apennines, and rocked the forest impotently. The moon went down; besides, the clouds, black with snow, now covered all the heaven.

The watcher could no longer watch; he could not see his own hand. Impatience spoke in him; he changed his plan, and creeping forward, came by degrees — he had measured the distance to an inch — to the edge of the clearing where the great oak stood on whose boughs the king had hanged the bodies of his victims eight or nine months earlier. He could see nothing and hear nothing; but he knew the king was there; he thought he detected something rhythmical which might be his pace. For about half an hour he kept still; the wind died down a little; and he could hear the king, who was singing to himself a savage hymn of war and triumph. Now snow began to fall thickly, and a silhouette was visible against the gray background. It grew bitter cold.

The watcher had not foreseen any of this. He had imagined the scene as it had been three months before, glowing in autumn beauty. The present murk seemed to him a direct miracle of Diana.

For now, he saw his opportunity. The king began to shiver with the cold; he laid his sword at the foot of the great oak, and swung his long arms upon his breast. It was pure inspiration for the other; he could see enough to be sure that the man's back was turned to him; he broke out and rushed on him, like a bull. The king turned by instinct, but too slowly, for his first thought had been to grasp his sword. Before he knew it, the sturdy lad had got him by the waist, and flung him far into the wood. For a second, he lay half stunned; then he picked himself up, only to find his assailant gone.

For he, the moment that the king's body left him free, had sprung into the air, caught at a bough of the great oak, and torn away a branch. With this trophy he had run madly through the darkness to the temple.

The king was on his feet in a flash; he picked up his sword and dashed in pursuit. But the shock had been great; and fear clutched at his heart. He stumbled as he ran, and fell once more. This time he knew pursuit was useless; he raised his sword, and cried aloud upon Diana.

Then, with drooping weapon, he went slowly and tragically towards the temple.

Part V

Nine days had passed. The weather was brilliantly cold and clear. Snow still lay on the ground, but the sun, already rejoicing to run his new race through the heavens, laughed gladly upon the terrace of the temple.

There was a great crowd of persons of all ranks; Rome had turned out in force to witness the event of the day.

On the steps of the temple stood a high official, surrounded by many patricians; by his side was the King of the Wood; alone, as one awaiting judgement, a few yards in front of him, stood the hero of the recent adventure.

"Romans!" proclaimed the official, turning from the little altar where he had inaugurated the proceedings by offering sacrifice to Diana. "Romans! we are here to investigate the claim made nine days ago by the slave Titus now here present before us to succeed to the honor, rank, and dignity of Priest to Diana our Lady, and King of the Wood. The conditions of succession are too familiar to all of you for me to weary you by repeating them. It is necessary that the claimant should be a runaway slave. Can this be testified?"

The husband of the Lady Clodia stepped forward. "The rascal is my slave," said he.

"And you did not sell him, or free him?" "The rogue ran away two days before I came back from victory. He had been insolent to the Lady of my house, and deserved a cudgeling. We shall soon know whether he did wisely."

"Good," replied the orator. "The second essential is that unarmed he should have surprised the vigilance of the King of the Wood, and plucked a bough from the sacred oak of Diana. I have personally compared this bough, presented by the slave Titus, with the holy tree; and it was certainly torn thence by him in the approved manner. The King admits that Titus had no weapon, as by his oath

142

before Diana he was bound. The third condition is that the slave should conquer the King in single combat. Are you ready for the battle?"

"With no less ambition would I have left so noble, kind, and excellent a master," replied Titus firmly, lifting the sword that Clodia had given him.

"That's truth enough," laughed her husband, "for there's my missing sword! Well, be fortunate as you are brave!" he added kindly. Clodia took the opportunity; she gave a sidelong smile. The youth's heart leapt higher than ever; from that moment he knew he could not fail.

"Let us proceed!" exclaimed the official, and led the way to the sacred oak.

The battle was not of long duration. The elder man had lost his nerve; the nine days of preparation for the fight, so far from strengthening him, had weakened him. The omens had been continuously evil. He had never fought an armed man since the day he had won for himself the fatal office; and his predecessor had been an old gray man with feeble arm and failing sight. He knew no cunning of sword play; and Titus had taken care to boast that for three months he had been trained by the first masters in Rome. He could only hope to win by length of reach and speed of foot. The first blow would settle all, with deadly Roman swords and no defensive armor.

So, he leapt madly at Titus, who with quick eye caught the blade on his own, and, thrusting himself under the King's leap that lost him balance, he plunged his sword hilt-deep into the breast of his opponent, who fell dead without a word.

Instantly the populace broke into cries of joy. Titus, his bloody sword held high, was carried in triumph to the temple. "Hail, Priest of Diana!" they cried, "Hail, King of the Wood of Nemi!" The Roman ladies vied in their excitement to touch the sword; but

Clodia conquered. Willingly the new King lowered the blade, and let her slake her mouth on its red stain.

They brought the King finally to the shrine. There he offered his sword to Diana, and there he took before the people the vows of priest and king.

A month later Clodia's husband died, and, inconsolable, she became the devotee of Diana, making pilgrimages almost daily to the shrine.

So, Titus lived, and so she lived, in that base imitation of true happiness which sin sometimes vouchsafes to those who do not understand that a pure and noble life is the sole key to felicity. So, they lived, many a year, until — Until? That happened which always happened on the fair land that lies about

"The still glassy lake that lies

Beneath Aricia's trees —

Those trees in whose dim shadow

The ghastly priest doth reign,

The priest who slew the slayer,

And shall himself be slain."

Indeed, their love was sealed a second time in blood.

(Author's note. In writing this story, I have borrowed a few epithets and even phrases from Dr. J. G. Frazer's *Golden Bough*. My story obliged me to describe the scene of the tragedy, and it would have been presumptuous, and have exposed me to ridicule, had I attempted to rival his magical prose. To borrow seemed the lesser crime.)

Aphorisms From the East

by Helena P. Blavatsky

The glamour of Time conceals from the weak souls of men the dark abysses around them, the terrible and mighty laws which incessantly direct their lives.

-oOo-

There is no death without sin, and no affliction without transgression.

-oOo-

Man's actions are divided, as regards their object, into four classes; they are either *purposeless, unimportant,* or *vain,* or *good.*

-oOo-

The sun causes day and night, divine and human. Night is for the sleep of beings, day for the performance of their duty.

-oOo-

If we were convinced that we could never make our crooked ways straight, we should forever continue in our errors.

-oOo-

Where there are not virtue and discrimination, learning is not to be sown there, no more than good seed in barren soil.

-oOo-

A teacher is more venerable than ten sub-teachers; a father, than one hundred teachers; a mother, than a thousand fathers.

-oOo-

Let not a man, even though pained, be sour-tempered, nor devise a deed of mischief to another.

-oOo-

One is not aged because his head is grey: whoever, although a youth, has wisdom, him the gods consider an elder.

-oOo-

A wise man should ever shrink from honor as from poison, and should always be desirous of disrespect as if of ambrosia.

-oOo-

Though despised, one sleeps with comfort, with comfort awakes, with comfort lives in this world; but the scorner perisheth.

-oOo-

Trust not in business one ever caught asleep by the sun rising or setting, for thereby he incurs great sin.

-oOo-

Those who prefer to swim in the waters of their ignorance, and to go down very low, need not exert the body or heart; they need only cease to move, and they will surely sink.

-oOo-

As a man digging comes to water, so a zealous student attains unto knowledge.

-oOo-

A good man may receive pure knowledge even from an inferior; the highest virtue from the lowest.

-oOo-

Ambrosia may be extracted even from poison; elegant speech even from a fool; virtue even from an enemy; and gold from dross.

-oOo-

Whoever offers not food to the poor, raiment to the naked, and consolation to the afflicted, is reborn poor, naked, and suffering.

-oOo-

As a sower gets not his harvest if he sow seed in salt soil, so the giver gets no fruit by bestowing on the unworthy.

-oOo-

There are three things of which one never tires: health, life and wealth.

-oOo-

A misfortune that cometh from on high cannot be averted; caution is useless against the decrees of Fate.

-oOo-

The worst of maladies is envy; the best of medicines is health.

-oOo-

Three things can never be got with three things: wealth, with wishing for it; youth, with cosmetics; health, with medicine.

-oOo-

Trifling ruins earnestness, lying is the enemy of truth, and oppression perverts justice.

-oOo-

Caution can never incur disgrace; imbecility can never bring honor with it.

-oOo-

Whomsoever riches do not exalt, poverty will not abase, nor calamity cast him down.

-oOo-

Night and day are the steeds of man; they hurry him on, not he them.

-oOo-

Whoso heeds not a plaint, confesses his own meanness; and whoso makes a merit of his charity, incurs reproach.

-oOo-

There are four things of which a little goes on a long way: pain, poverty, error, and enmity.

-oOo-

He who knows not his own worth, will never appreciate the worth of others.

-oOo-

Whosoever is ashamed of his father and mother, is excluded from the ranks of the wise.

-oOo-

He who is not lowly in his own sight, will never be exalted in the sight of others.

The Demon Pope

by Richard Garnett

"So you won't sell me your soul?" said the devil.

"Thank you," replied the student, "I had rather keep it myself, if it's all the same to you."

"But it's not all the same to me. I want it very particularly. Come, I'll be liberal. I said twenty years. You can have thirty."

The student shook his head.

"Forty!"

Another shake.

"Fifty!"

As before.

"Now," said the devil, "I know I'm going to do a foolish thing, but I cannot bear to see a clever, spirited young man throw himself away. I'll make you another kind of offer. We won't have any bargain at present, but I will push you on in the world for the next forty years. This day forty years I come back and ask you for a boon; not your soul, mind, or anything not perfectly in your power to grant. If you give it, we are quits; if not, I fly away with you. What say you to this?"

The student reflected for some minutes. "Agreed," he said at last.

Scarcely had the devil disappeared, which he did instantaneously, ere a messenger reined in his smoking steed at the gate of the University of Cordova (the judicious reader will already have remarked that Lucifer could never have been allowed inside a Christian seat of learning), and, inquiring for the student Gerbert, presented him with the Emperor Otho's nomination to the Abbacy

149

of Bobbio, in consideration, said the document, of his virtue and learning, well-nigh miraculous in one so young. Such messengers were frequent visitors during Gerbert's prosperous career. Abbot, bishop, archbishop, cardinal, he was ultimately enthroned Pope on April 2, 999, and assumed the appellation of Silvester the Second. It was then a general belief that the world would come to an end in the following year, a catastrophe which to many seemed the more imminent from the election of a chief pastor whose celebrity as a theologian, though not inconsiderable, by no means equaled his reputation as a necromancer.

The world, notwithstanding, revolved scathless through the dreaded twelvemonth, and early in the first year of the eleventh century Gerbert was sitting peacefully in his study, perusing a book of magic. Volumes of algebra, astrology, alchemy, Aristotelian philosophy, and other such light reading filled his bookcase; and on a table stood an improved clock of his invention, next to his introduction of the Arabic numerals his chief legacy to posterity. Suddenly a sound of wings was heard, and Lucifer stood by his side.

"It is a long time," said the fiend, "since I have had the pleasure of seeing you. I have now called to remind you of our little contract, concluded this day forty years."

"You remember," said Silvester, "that you are not to ask anything exceeding my power to perform."

"I have no such intention," said Lucifer. "On the contrary, I am about to solicit a favor which can be bestowed by you alone. You are Pope, I desire that you would make me a Cardinal."

"In the expectation, I presume," returned Gerbert, "of becoming Pope on the next vacancy."

"An expectation," replied Lucifer, "which I may most reasonably entertain, considering my enormous wealth, my proficiency in intrigue, and the present condition of the Sacred College."

"You would doubtless," said Gerbert, "endeavor to subvert the foundations of the Faith, and, by a course of profligacy and

150

licentiousness, render the Holy See odious and contemptible."

"On the contrary," said the fiend, "I would extirpate heresy, and all learning and knowledge as inevitably tending thereunto. I would suffer no man to read but the priest, and confine his reading to his breviary. I would burn your books together with your bones on the first convenient opportunity. I would observe an austere propriety of conduct, and be especially careful not to loosen one rivet in the tremendous yoke I was forging for the minds and consciences of mankind."

"If it be so," said Gerbert, "let's be off!"

"What!" exclaimed Lucifer, "you are willing to accompany me to the infernal regions!"

"Assuredly, rather than be accessory to the burning of Plato and Aristotle, and give place to the darkness against which I have been contending all my life."

"Gerbert," replied the demon, "this is arrant trifling. Know you not that no good man can enter my dominions? that, were such a thing possible, my empire would become intolerable to me, and I should be compelled to abdicate?"

"I do know it," said Gerbert, "and hence I have been able to receive your visit with composure."

"Gerbert," said the devil, with tears in his eyes, "I put it to you—is this fair, is this honest? I undertake to promote your interests in the world; I fulfill my promise abundantly. You obtain through my instrumentality a position to which you could never otherwise have aspired. Often have I had a hand in the election of a Pope, but never before have I contributed to confer the tiara on one eminent for virtue and learning. You profit by my assistance to the full, and now take advantage of an adventitious circumstance to deprive me of my reasonable guerdon. It is my constant experience that the good people are much more slippery than the sinners, and drive much harder bargains."

"Lucifer," answered Gerbert, " I have always sought to treat you as a gentleman, hoping that you would approve yourself such in return. I will not inquire whether it was entirely in harmony with this character to seek to intimidate me into compliance with your demand by threatening me with a penalty which you well knew could not be enforced. I will overlook this little irregularity, and concede even more than you have requested. You have asked to be a Cardinal. I will make you Pope"

"Ha!" exclaimed Lucifer, and an internal glow suffused his sooty hide, as the light of a fading ember is revived by breathing upon it.

"For twelve hours," continued Gerbert. "At the expiration of that time we will consider the matter further; and if, as I anticipate, you are more anxious to divest yourself of the Papal dignity than you were to assume it, I promise to bestow upon you any boon you may ask within my power to grant, and not plainly inconsistent with religion or morals."

"Done!" cried the demon. Gerbert uttered some cabalistic words, and in a moment the apartment held two Pope Silvesters, entirely indistinguishable save by their attire, and the fact that one limped slightly with the left foot.

"You will find the Pontifical apparel in this cupboard," said Gerbert, and, taking his book of magic with him, he retreated through a masked door to a secret chamber. As the door closed behind him he chuckled, and muttered to himself, "Poor old Lucifer! Sold again!"

If Lucifer was sold he did not seem to know it. He approached a large slab of silver which did duty as a mirror, and contemplated his personal appearance with some dissatisfaction.

"I certainly don't look half so well without my horns," he soliloquized, "and I am sure I shall miss my tail most grievously."

A tiara and a train, however, made fair amends for the deficient appendages, and Lucifer now looked every inch a Pope. He was about to call the master of the ceremonies, and summon a consistory, when the door was burst open, and seven cardinals, brandishing poniards, rushed into the room.

"Down with the sorcerer!" they cried, as they seized and gagged him. "Death to the Saracen!" "Practices algebra, and other devilish arts!" "Knows Greek!" "Talks Arabic!" "Reads Hebrew!" "Burn him!" "Smother him!"

"Let him be deposed by a general council," said a young and inexperienced cardinal.

"Heaven forbid!" said an old and wary one, *sotto voce*.

Lucifer struggled frantically, but the feeble frame he was doomed to inhabit for the next eleven hours was speedily exhausted. Bound and helpless, he swooned away.

"Brethren," said one of the senior cardinals, "it hath been delivered by the exorcists that a sorcerer or other individual in league with the demon doth usually bear upon his person some visible token of his infernal compact. I propose that we forthwith institute a search for this stigma, the discovery of which may contribute to justify our proceedings in the eyes of the world."

"I heartily approve of our brother Anno's proposition," said another, "the rather as we cannot possibly fail to discover such a mark, if, indeed, we desire to find it."

The search was accordingly instituted, and had not proceeded far ere a simultaneous yell from all the seven cardinals indicated that their investigation had brought more to light than they had ventured to expect.

The Holy Father had a cloven foot!

For the next five minutes the cardinals remained utterly stunned, silent, and stupefied with amazement. As they gradually recovered their faculties it would have become manifest to a nice observer that the Pope had risen very considerably in their good opinion.

"This is an affair requiring very mature deliberation," said one.

"I always feared that we might be proceeding too precipitately," said another.

"It is written, 'the devils believe,'" said a third: "the Holy Father, therefore, is not a heretic at any rate."

"Brethren," said Anno, "this affair, as our brother Benno well remarks, doth indeed call for mature deliberation. I therefore propose that, instead of smothering his Holiness with cushions, as originally contemplated, we immure him for the present in the dungeon adjoining hereunto, and, after spending the night in meditation and prayer, resume the consideration of the business tomorrow morning."

"Informing the officials of the palace," said Benno, "that his Holiness has retired for his devotions, and desires on no account to be disturbed."

"A pious fraud," said Anno, "which not one of the Fathers would for a moment have scrupled to commit."

The Cardinals accordingly lifted the still insensible Lucifer, and bore him carefully, almost tenderly, to the apartment appointed for his detention. Each would fain have lingered in hopes of his recovery, but each felt that the eyes of his six brethren were upon him: and all, therefore, retired simultaneously, each taking a key of the cell.

Lucifer regained consciousness almost immediately afterwards. He had the most confused idea of the circumstances which had involved him in his present scrape, and could only say to himself that if they were the usual concomitants of the Papal dignity, these were by no means to his taste, and he wished he had been made acquainted with them sooner. The dungeon was not only perfectly dark, but horribly cold, and the poor devil in his present form had no latent store of infernal heat to draw upon. His teeth chattered, he shivered in every limb, and felt devoured with hunger and thirst. There is much probability in the assertion of some of his biographers that it was on this occasion that he invented ardent spirits; but, even if he did, the mere conception of a glass of brandy could only increase his sufferings. So the long January night wore wearily on, and Lucifer seemed likely to expire from inanition, when a key turned in the lock, and Cardinal Anno cautiously glided in, bearing a lamp, a loaf, half a cold roast kid, and a bottle of wine.

"I trust," he said, bowing courteously, "that I may be excused any slight breach of etiquette of which I may render myself culpable from the difficulty under which I labor of determining whether, under present circumstances, 'Your Holiness,' or 'Your Infernal Majesty' be the form of address most befitting me to employ."

"Bub-ub-bub-boo," went Lucifer, who still had the gag in his mouth.

"Heavens!" exclaimed the Cardinal, "I crave your Infernal Holiness's forgiveness. What a lamentable oversight!"

And, relieving Lucifer from his gag and bonds, he set out the refection, upon which the demon fell voraciously.

"Why the devil, if I may so express myself," pursued Anno, "did not your Holiness inform us that you *were* the devil? Not a hand would then have been raised against you. I have myself been seeking all my life for the audience now happily vouchsafed me. Whence this mistrust of your faithful Anno, who has served you so loyally and zealously these many years?"

Lucifer pointed significantly to the gag and fetters.

"I shall never forgive myself," protested the Cardinal, "for the part I have borne in this unfortunate transaction. Next to ministering to your Majesty's bodily necessities, there is nothing I have so much at heart as to express my penitence. But I entreat your Majesty to remember that I believed myself to be acting in your Majesty's interest by overthrowing a magician who was accustomed to send your Majesty upon errands, and who might at any time enclose you in a box, and cast you into the sea. It is deplorable that your Majesty's most devoted servants should have been thus misled."

"Reasons of State," suggested Lucifer.

"I trust that they no longer operate," said the Cardinal. "However, the Sacred College is now fully possessed of the whole matter: it is therefore unnecessary to pursue this department of the subject further. I would now humbly crave leave to confer with your Majesty, or rather, perhaps, your Holiness, since I am about to speak of spiritual things, on the important and delicate point of your Holiness's successor. I am ignorant how long your Holiness proposes to occupy the Apostolic chair; but of course you are aware that public opinion will not suffer you to hold it for a term exceeding that of the pontificate of Peter. A vacancy, therefore, must one day occur; and I am humbly to represent that the office could not be filled by one more congenial than myself to the present incumbent, or on whom he could more fully rely to carry out in every respect his views and intentions."

And the Cardinal provided to detail various circumstances of his past life, which certainly seemed to corroborate his assertion. He had not, however, proceeded far ere he was disturbed by the grating of another key in the lock, and had just time to whisper impressively, "Beware of Benno," ere he dived under a table.

Benno was also provided with a lamp, wine, and cold viands. Warned by the other lamp and the remains of Lucifer's repast that some colleague had been beforehand with him, and not knowing how many more might be in the field, he came briefly to the point as regarded the Papacy, and preferred his claim in much the same manner as Anno. While he was earnestly cautioning Lucifer against this Cardinal as one who could and would cheat the very Devil himself, another key turned in the lock, and Benno escaped under the table, where Anno immediately inserted his finger into his right eye. The little squeal consequent upon this occurrence Lucifer successfully smothered by a fit of coughing.

Cardinal No. 3, a Frenchman, bore a Bayonne ham, and exhibited the same disgust as Benno on seeing himself forestalled. So far as his requests transpired they were moderate, but no one knows where he would have stopped if he had not been scared by the advent of Cardinal No. 4. Up to this time he had only asked for an inexhaustible purse, power to call up the Devil *ad libitum,* and a ring of invisibility to allow him free access to his mistress, who was unfortunately a married woman.

Cardinal No. 4 chiefly wanted to be put into the way of poisoning Cardinal No. 5; and Cardinal No. 5 preferred the same petition as respected Cardinal No. 4.

Cardinal No. 6, an Englishman, demanded the reversion of the Archbishoprics of Canterbury and York, with the faculty of holding them together, and of unlimited non-residence. In the course of his harangue he made use of the phrase *non obstantibus,* of which Lucifer immediately took a note.

What the seventh Cardinal would have solicited is not known, for he had hardly opened his mouth when the twelfth hour expired, and Lucifer, regaining his vigor with his shape, sent the Prince of the Church spinning to the other end of the room, and split the table with a single stroke of his tail. The six crouched and huddling Cardinals cowered revealed to one another, and at the same time enjoyed the spectacle of his Holiness darting through the stone ceiling, which yielded like a film to his passage, and closed up afterwards as if nothing had happened. After the first shock of dismay they unanimously rushed to the door, but found it bolted on the outside. There was no other exit, and no means of giving an alarm. In this emergency the demeanor of the Italian Cardinals set a bright example to their ultramontane colleagues. *"Bisogna pazienzia"* they said, as they shrugged their shoulders. Nothing could exceed the mutual politeness of Cardinals Anno and Benno, unless that of the two who had sought to poison each other. The Frenchman was held to have gravely derogated from good manners by alluding to this circumstance, which had reached his ears while he was under the table: and the Englishman swore so outrageously at the plight in which he found himself that the Italians then and there silently registered a vow that none of his nation should ever be Pope, a maxim which, with one exception, has been observed to this day.

Lucifer, meanwhile, had repaired to Silvester, whom he found arrayed in all the insignia of his dignity; of which, as he remarked, he thought his visitor had probably had enough.

"I should think so indeed," replied Lucifer. "But at the same time I feel myself fully repaid for all I have undergone by the assurance of the loyalty of my friends and admirers, and the conviction that it is needless for me to devote any considerable amount of personal attention to ecclesiastical affairs. I now claim the promised boon, which it will be in no way inconsistent with thy functions to grant, seeing that it is a work of mercy. I demand that the Cardinals be released, and that their conspiracy against thee, by which I alone suffered, be buried in oblivion."

"I hoped you would carry them all off," said Gerbert, with an expression of disappointment.

"Thank you," said the Devil. "It is more to my interest to leave them where they are."

So the dungeon-door was unbolted, and the Cardinals came forth, sheepish and crestfallen. If, after all, they did less mischief than Lucifer had expected from them, the cause was their entire bewilderment by what had passed, and their utter inability to penetrate the policy of Gerbert, who henceforth devoted himself even with ostentation to good works. They could never quite satisfy themselves whether they were speaking to the Pope or to the Devil, and when under the latter impression habitually emitted propositions which Gerbert justly stigmatized as rash, temerarious, and scandalous. They plagued him with allusions to certain matters mentioned in their interviews with Lucifer, with which they naturally but erroneously supposed him to be conversant, and worried him by continual nods and titterings as they glanced at his nether extremities. To abolish this nuisance, and at the same time silence sundry unpleasant rumors which had somehow got abroad, Gerbert devised the ceremony of kissing the Pope's feet, which, in a grievously mutilated form, endures to this day. The stupefaction of the Cardinals on discovering that the Holy Father had lost his hoof surpasses all description, and they went to their graves without having obtained the least insight into the mystery.

The Cedar Closet

by Lafcadio Hearn

It happened ten years ago, and it stands out, and ever will stand out, in my memory like some dark, awful barrier dividing the happy, gleeful years of girlhood, with their foolish, petulant sorrows and eager, innocent joys, and the bright, lovely life which has been mine since. In looking back, that time seems to me shadowed by a dark and terrible brooding cloud, bearing in its lurid gloom what, but for love and patience the tenderest and most untiring, might have been the bolt of death, or, worse a thousand times, of madness. As it was, for months after "life crept on a broken wing," if not "through cells of madness," yet verily "through haunts of horror and fear." O, the weary, weary days and months when I longed piteously for rest! when sunshine was torture, and every shadow filled with horror unspeakable; when my soul's craving was for death; to be allowed to creep away from the terror which lurked in the softest murmur of the summer breeze, the flicker of the shadow of the tiniest leaf on the sunny grass, in every corner and curtain-fold in my dear old home. But love conquered all, and I can tell my story now, with awe and wonder, it is true, but quietly and calmly.

Ten years ago, I was living with my only brother in one of the quaint, ivy-grown, red-gabled rectories which are so picturesquely scattered over the fair breadth of England. We were orphans, Archibald and I; and I had been the busy, happy mistress of his pretty home for only one year after leaving school, when Robert Draye asked me to be his wife. Robert and Archie were old friends, and my new home, Draye's Court, was only separated from the parsonage by an old gray wall, a low iron-studded door in which admitted us from the sunny parsonage dawn to the old, old park which had belonged to the Drayes for centuries. Robert was lord of the manor; and it was he who had given Archie the living of Draye in the Wold.

It was the night before my wedding day, and our pretty home was crowded with the wedding guests. We were all gathered in the large old-fashioned drawing-room after dinner. When Robert left us late in the evening, I walked with him, as usual, to the little gate for what he called our last parting; we lingered awhile under the great walnut-tree, through the heavy, somber branches of which the September moon poured its soft pure light. With his last good-night kiss on my lips and my heart full of him and the love which warmed and glorified the whole world for me, I did not care to go back to share in the fun and frolic in the drawing-room, but went softly upstairs to my own room. I say "my own room," but I was to occupy it as a bedroom tonight for the first time. It was a pleasant south room, wainscoted in richly-carved cedar, which gave the atmosphere a spicy fragrance. I had chosen it as my morning room on my arrival in our home; here I had read and sang and painted, and spent long, sunny hours while Archibald was busy in his study after breakfast. I had had a bed arranged there as I preferred being alone to sharing my own larger bedroom with two of my bridesmaids. It looked bright and cozy as I came in; my favorite low chair was drawn before the fire, whose rosy light glanced and flickered on the glossy dark walls, which gave the room its name, "The Cedar Closet." My maid was busy preparing my toilet table, I sent her away, and sat down to wait for my brother, who I knew would come to bid me goodnight. He came; we had our last fireside talk in my girlhood's home; and when he left me there was an incursion of all my bridesmaids for a "dressing-gown reception."

When at last I was alone I drew back the curtain and curled myself up on the low wide window-seat. The moon was at its brightest; the little church and quiet churchyard beyond the lawn looked fair and calm beneath its rays; the gleam of the white headstones here and there between the trees might have reminded me that life is not all peace and joy--that tears and pain, fear and parting, have their share in its story--but it did not. The tranquil happiness with which my heart was full overflowed in some soft tears which had no tinge of bitterness, and when at last I did lie down, peace, deep and perfect, still seemed to flow in on me with the moonbeams which filled the room, shimmering on the folds of my bridal dress, which was laid ready for the morning. I am thus minute in describing my last waking moments, that it may be understood that what followed was not creation of a morbid fancy.

I do not know how long I had been asleep, when I was suddenly, as it were, wrenched back to consciousness. The moon had set, the room was quite dark; I could just distinguish the glimmer of a clouded, starless sky through the open window. I could not see or hear anything unusual, but not the less was I conscious of an unwonted, a baleful presence near; an indescribable horror cramped the very beatings of my heart; with every instant the certainty grew that my room was shared by some evil being. I could not cry for help, though Archie's room was so close, and I knew that one call through the death-like stillness would bring him to me; all I could do was to gaze, gaze, gaze into the darkness. Suddenly--and a throb stung through every nerve--I heard distinctly from behind the wainscot against which the head of my bed was placed a low, hollow moan, followed on the instant by a cackling, malignant laugh from the other side of the room. If I had been one of the monumental figures in the little churchyard on which I had seen the quiet moonbeams shine a few hours before I could not have been more utterly unable to move or speak; every other faculty seemed to be lost in the one intent strain of eye and ear. There came at last the sound of a halting step, the tapping of a crutch upon the floor, then stillness, and slowly, gradually the room filled with light--a pale, cold, steady light. Everything around was exactly as I had last seen it in the mingled shine of the moon and fire, and though I heard at intervals the harsh laugh, the curtain at the foot of the bed hid from me whatever uttered it. Again, low but distinct, the piteous moan broke forth, followed by some words in a foreign tongue, and with the sound a figure started from behind the curtain--a dwarfed, deformed woman, dressed in a loose robe of black, sprinkled with golden stars, which gave forth a dull, fiery gleam, in the mysterious light; one lean, yellow hand clutched the curtain of my bed; it glittered with jeweled rings;--long black hair fell in heavy masses from a golden circlet over the stunted form. I saw it all clearly as I now see the pen which writes these words and the hand which guides it. The face was turned from me, bent aside, as if greedily drinking in those astonished moans; I noted even the streaks of gray in the long tresses, as I lay helpless in dumb, bewildered horror.

"Again!" she said hoarsely, as the sounds died away into indistinct murmurs, and advancing a step she tapped sharply with a crutch on the cedar wainscot; then again louder and more purposeful rose the wild beseeching voice; this time the words were English.

"Mercy, have mercy! not on me, but on my child, my little one; she never harmed you. She is dying--she is dying here in darkness; let me but see her face once more. Death is very near, nothing can save her now; but grant one ray of light, and I will pray that you may be forgiven, if forgiveness there be for such as you."

"What, you kneel at last! Kneel to Gerda, and kneel in vain. A ray of light; Not if you could pay for it in diamonds. You are mine! Shriek and call as you will, no other ears can hear. Die together. You are mine to torture as I will; mine, mine, mine!" and again an awful laugh rang through the room. At the instant she turned. O the face of malign horror that met my gaze! The green eyes flamed, and with something like the snarl of a savage beast she sprang toward me; that hideous face almost touched mine; the grasp of the skinny jeweled hand was all but on me; then--I suppose I fainted.

For weeks I lay in brain fever, in mental horror and weariness so intent, that even now I do not like to let my mind dwell on it. Even when the crisis was safely past I was slow to rally; my mind was utterly unstrung. I lived in a world of shadows. And so winter wore by, and brought us to the fair spring morning when at last I stood by Robert's side in the old church, a cold, passive, almost unwilling bride. I cared neither to refuse nor consent to anything that was suggested; so Robert and Archie decided for me, and I allowed them to do with me as they would, while I brooded silently and ceaselessly on the memory of that terrible night. To my husband I told all one morning in a sunny Bavarian valley, and my weak, frightened mind drew strength and peace from his; by degrees the haunting horror wore away, and when we came home for a happy reason nearly two years afterward, I was as strong and blithe as in my girlhood. I had learned to believe that it had all been, not the cause, but the commencement of my fever. I was to be undeceived.

Our little daughter had come to us in the time of roses; and now Christmas was with us, our first Christmas at home, and the house was full of guests. It was a delicious old-fashioned Yule; plenty of skating and outdoor fun, and no lack of brightness indoors. Toward New Year a heavy fall of snow set in which kept us all prisoners; but even then the days flew merrily, and somebody suggested tableaux for the evenings. Robert was elected manager; there was a debate and selection of subjects, and then came the puzzle of where, at such short notice, we could procure the dresses required. My husband advised a raid on some mysterious oaken chests which he knew had been for years stowed away in a turret-room. He remembered having, when a boy, seen the housekeeper inspecting them, and their contents had left a hazy impression of old stand-alone brocades, gold tissues, sacques, hoops, and hoods, the very mention of which put us in a state of wild excitement. Mrs. Moultrie was summoned, looked duly horrified at the desecration of what to her were relics most sacred; but seeing it was inevitable, she marshaled the way, a protest in every rustle and fold of her stiff silk dress.

"What a charming old place," was the exclamation with variations as we entered the long oak-joisted room, at the further end of which stood in goodly array the chests whose contents we coveted. Bristling with unspoken disapproval, poor Mrs. Moultrie unlocked one after another, and then asked permission to retire, leaving us unchecked to "cry havoc." In a moment the floor was covered with piles of silks and velvets.

"Meg," cried little Janet Crawford, dancing up to me, "isn't it a good thing to live in the age of tulle and summer silks? Fancy being imprisoned for life in a fortress like this!" holding up a thick crimson and gold brocade, whale-boned and buckramed at all points. It was thrown aside, and she half lost herself in another chest and was silent. Then--"Look, Major Fraudel This is the very thing for you--a true astrologer's robe, all black velvet and golden stars. If it were but long enough; it just fits me."

I turned and saw--the pretty slight figure, the innocent girlish face dressed in the robe of black and gold, identical in shape, pattern and material with what I too well remembered. With a wild cry I hid my face and cowered away.

"Take it off! O, Janet--Robert--take it from her!"

Every one turned wondering. In an instant my husband saw, and catching up the cause of my terror, flung it hastily into the chest again, and lowered the lid. Janet looked half offended, but the cloud passed in an instant when I kissed her, apologizing as well as I could. Rob laughed at us both, and voted an adjournment to a warmer room, where we could have the chests brought to us to ransack at leisure. Before going down, Janet and I went into a small anteroom to examine some old pictures which leaned against the wall.

"This is just the thing, Jennie, to frame the tableaux," I said, pointing to an immense frame, at least twelve feet square. "There is a picture in it," I added, pulling back the dusty folds of a heavy curtain which fell before it.

"That can be easily removed," said my husband, who had followed us.

With his assistance we drew the curtain quite away, and in the now fast waning light could just discern the figure of a girl in white against a dark background. Robert rang for a lamp, and when it came we turned with much curiosity to examine the painting, as to the subject of which we had been making odd merry guesses while we waited. The girl was young, almost childish--very lovely, but, oh, how sad! Great tears stood in the innocent eyes and on the round young cheeks, and her hands were clasped tenderly around the arms of a man who was bending toward her, and, did I dream?--no, there in hateful distinctness was the hideous woman of the

Cedar Closet--the same in every distorted line, even to the starred dress and golden circlet. The swarthy hues of the dress and face had at first caused us to overlook her. The same wicked eyes seemed to glare into mine. After one wild bound my heart seemed to stop its beating, and I knew no more. When I recovered from a long, deep swoon, great lassitude and intense nervous excitement followed; my illness broke up the party, and for months I was an invalid. When again Robert's love and patience had won me back to my old health and happiness, he told me all the truth, so far as it had been preserved in old records of the family

It was in the sixteenth century that the reigning lady of Draye Court was a weird, deformed woman, whose stunted body, hideous face, and a temper which taught her to hate and vilify everything good and beautiful for the contrast offered to herself, made her universally feared and disliked. One talent only she possessed; it was for music; but so wild and strange were the strains she drew from the many instruments of which she was mistress, that the gift only intensified the dread with which she was regarded. Her father had died before her birth; her mother did not survive it; near relatives she had none; she had lived her lonely, loveless life from youth to middle age. When a young girl came to the Court, no one knew more than that she was a poor relation. The dark woman seemed to look more kindly on this young cousin than on any one that had hitherto crossed her somber path, and indeed so great was the charm which Marian's goodness, beauty and innocent gayety exercised on every one that the servants ceased to marvel at her having gained the favor of their gloomy mistress. The girl seemed to feel a kind of wondering, pitying affection for the unhappy woman; she looked on her through an atmosphere created by her own sunny nature, and for a time all went well. When Marian had been at the Court for a year, a foreign musician appeared on the scene. He was a Spaniard, and had been engaged by Lady Draye to build for her an organ said to be of fabulous power and sweetness. Through long bright summer days he and his employer were shut up together in the music-room--he busy in the construction of the wonderful instrument, she aiding and watching his work. These days were spent by Marian in various ways--pleasant idleness and pleasant work, long canters on her chestnut pony, dreamy mornings by the brook with rod and line, or in the village near, where she found a welcome everywhere. She played with the children, nursed the babies, helped the mothers in a thousand pretty ways, gossiped with old people, brightening the day for everybody with whom she came in contact. Then in the evening she sat with Lady Draye and the Spaniard in the saloon talking in that soft foreign tongue which they generally used. But this was but the music between the acts; the terrible drama was coming. The motive was of course the same as that of every life drama which has been played out from the old, old days when the curtain rose upon the garden scene of Paradise. Philip and Marian loved each other, and having told their happy secret to each other, they, as in duty bound, took it to their patroness. They found her in the music room. Whether the glimpses she caught of a beautiful world from which she was shut out maddened her, or whether she, too, loved the foreigner, was never certainly known; but through the closed door, passionate words were heard, and very soon Philip came out alone, and left the house without a farewell to any in it. When the servants did at last venture to enter, they found Marian lifeless on the floor, Lady Draye standing over her with crutch uplifted, and blood flowing from a wound in the girl's forehead. They carried her away and nursed her tenderly; their mistress locked the door as they left, and all night long remained alone in darkness. The music which came out without pause on the still night air was weird and wicked beyond any strains which had ever before flowed even from beneath her fingers; it ceased with morning light; and as the day wore on it was found that Marian had fled during the night, and that Philip's organ had sounded its last strain--Lady Draye had shattered and silenced it forever. She never seemed to notice Marian's absence and no one dared to mention her name. Nothing was ever known certainly of her fate; it was supposed that she had joined her lover.

Years passed, and with each Lady Draye's temper grew fiercer and more malevolent. She never quitted her room unless on the anniversary of that day and night, when the tapping of her crutch and high-heeled shoes was heard for hours as she walked up and down the music-room, which was never entered save for this yearly vigil. The tenth anniversary came round, and this time the vigil was not unshared. The servants distinctly heard the sound of a man's voice mingling in earnest conversation with her shrill tones; they listened long, and at last one of the boldest ventured to look in, himself unseen. He saw a worn, traveled-stained man; dusty, foot-sore, poorly dressed, he still at once recognized the handsome, gay Philip of ten years ago. He held in his arms a little sleeping girl; her long curls, so like poor Marian's, strayed over his shoulder. He seemed to be pleading in that strange musical tongue for the little one; for as he spoke he lifted, O, so tenderly, the cloak which partly concealed her, and showed the little face, which he doubtless thought might plead for itself. The woman, with a furious gesture, raised her crutch to strike the child; he stepped quickly backward, stooped to kiss the little girl, then, without a word, turned to go. Lady Draye called on him to return with an imperious gesture, spoke a few words, to which he seemed to listen gratefully, and together they left the house by the window which opened on the terrace. The servants followed them, and found she led the way to the parsonage, which was at the time unoccupied. It was said that he was in some political danger as well as in deep poverty, and that she had hidden him here until she could help him to a better asylum. It was certain that for many nights she went to the parsonage and returned before dawn, thinking herself unseen. But one morning she did not come home; her people consulted together; her relenting toward Philip had made them feel more kindly toward her than ever before; they sought her at the parsonage and found her lying across its threshold dead, a vial clasped in her rigid fingers. There was no sign of the late presence of Philip and his child; it was believed she had sped them on their way before she killed herself. They laid her in a suicide's grave. For more than fifty years after the parsonage was shut up. Though it had been again inhabited no one had ever been terrified by the specter I had seen; probably the Cedar Closet had never before been used as a bedroom.

Robert decided on having the wing containing the haunted room pulled down and rebuilt, and in doing so the truth of my story gained a horrible confirmation. When the wainscot of the Cedar Closet was removed a recess was discovered in the massive old wall, and in this lay moldering fragments of the skeletons of a man and child!

There could be but one conclusion drawn, the wicked woman had imprisoned them there under pretense of hiding and helping them; and once they were completely at her mercy, had come night after night with unimaginable cruelty to gloat over their agony, and, when that long anguish was ended, ended her odious life by a suicide's death. We could learn nothing of the mysterious painting. Philip was an artist, and it may have been his work. We had it destroyed, so that no record of the terrible story might remain. I have no more to add, save that but for those dark days left by Lady Draye as a legacy of fear and horror, I should never have known so well the treasure I hold in the tender, unwearying, faithful love of my husband--known the blessing that every sorrow carries in its heart, that

> "Every cloud that spreads above
> And veileth love, itself is love."

End.

Non-Human Inhabitants of the Astral Plane

by C. W. Leadbeater

It might have been thought fairly obvious, even to the most casual glance, that many of the terrestrial arrangements of Nature which affect us most nearly have not been designed exclusively with a view to our comfort, to even our ultimate advantage. Yet it was probably unavoidable that the human race, at least in its childhood, should imagine that this world and everything it contains existed solely for its own use and benefit; but undoubtedly we ought by this time to have grown out of that infantile delusion and realized our proper position and the duties that attach to it.

That most of us have not yet done so is shown in a dozen ways in our daily life – notably by the atrocious cruelty habitually displayed towards the animal kingdom under the name of sport by many who probably consider themselves highly civilized people. The veriest tyro in the holy science of occultism knows that all life is sacred and that without universal compassion there is no true progress; but it is only as he advances in his studies that he discovers how manifold evolution is, and how comparatively small a place humanity really fills in the economy of Nature.

It becomes clear to him that as earth, air, and water support myriads of forms of life which, though invisible to the ordinary eye, are revealed to us by the microscope, so the higher planes connected with our earth have an equally dense population of whose existence we are ordinarily completely unconscious. As his knowledge increases, he becomes more and more certain that in one way or another the utmost use is being made of every possibility of evolution, and that wherever it seems to us that in Nature force is being wasted or opportunity neglected, it is not the scheme of the universe that is in fault, but our ignorance of its method and intention.

For the purposes of our present consideration of the non-human inhabitants of the astral plane it will be best to leave altogether out of consideration those early forms of the universal life which are evolving, in a manner of which we can have little comprehension, through the successive encasement of atoms, molecules, and cells. If we commence at the lowest of what are usually called the elemental kingdoms, we shall even then have to group together under this general heading an enormous number of inhabitants of the astral plane upon whom it will be possible to touch only slightly, as anything like a detailed account of them would swell this manual to the dimensions of an encyclopedia.

The most convenient method of arranging the non-human entities will perhaps be in four classes – it being understood that in this case the class is not, as previously, a comparatively small subdivision, but usually a great kingdom of Nature at least as large and varied as, say, the animal or vegetable kingdom. Some of these classes rank considerably below humanity, some are our equals, and others again rise far above us in goodness and power. Some belong to our scheme of evolution – that is to say, they either have been or will be men like ourselves; others are evolving on entirely distinct lines of their own.

Before proceeding to consider them it is necessary in order to avoid the charge of incompleteness, to mention that in this branch of the subject two reservations have been made. First, no reference is made to the occasional appearances of high Adepts from other planets of the solar system and of even more august Visitors from a still greater distance, since such matters cannot fitly be described in an essay for general reading; and besides it is practically inconceivable, though theoretically possible, that such glorified Beings should ever need to manifest themselves on a plane so low as the astral. If for any reason they should wish to do so, the body appropriate to the plane would be temporarily created out of astral matter belonging to this planet, as in the case of the Nirmanakaya.

Secondly, quite outside of and entirely unconnected with the four classes into which we are dividing this section, there are two other great evolutions which at present share the use of this planet with humanity; but about them it is forbidden to give any particulars at this stage of the proceedings, as it is not apparently intended under ordinary circumstances either that they should be conscious of man's existence or man of theirs. If we ever do come into contact with them it will most probably be on the purely physical plane, for in any case their connection with our astral plane is of the slightest since the only possibility of their appearance there depends upon an extremely improbable accident in an act of ceremonial magic, which fortunately only a few of the most advanced sorcerers know how to perform. Nevertheless, that improbable accident has happened at least once, and may happen again, so that but for the prohibition above mentioned it would have been necessary to include them in our list.

1. *The Elemental Essence belonging to our own evolution.* As the name "elementary" has been given indiscriminately by various writers to any or all of man's possible *post-mortem* conditions, so this word "elemental" has been used at different times to mean any or all non-human spirits, from the most god-like of the Devas down through every variety of nature-spirit to the formless essence which pervades the kingdoms lying behind the mineral, until after reading several books the student becomes absolutely bewildered by the contradictory statements made on the subject. For the purposes of this treatise let it be understood that elemental essence is merely a name applied during certain stages of its evolution to monadic essence, which in its turn may be defined as the outpouring of Spirit or Divine Force into matter.

We are all familiar with the idea that before this outpouring arrives at the stage of individualization at which it forms the causal body of man, it has passed through and ensouled in turn six lower phases of evolution – the animal, vegetable, mineral, and three elemental kingdoms. When energizing through those respective stages it has sometimes been called the animal, vegetable, or mineral monad – though this term is distinctly misleading, since long before it arrives at any of these kingdoms it has become not *one*, but *many* monads. The name was, however, adopted to convey the idea that, though differentiation in the monadic essence had already long ago set in, it had not yet been carried to the extent of individualization.

When this monadic essence is energizing through the three great elemental kingdoms which precede the mineral, it is called by the name of "elemental essence." Before, however, its nature and the manner in which it manifests can be understood, the method in which spirit enfolds itself in its descent into matter must be realized.

Be it remembered, then, that when spirit resting on any plane (it matters not which – let us call it plane No. 1) wills to descend to the plane next below (let us call that plane No. 2) it must enfold itself in the matter of that plane – that is to say, it must draw round itself a veil of the matter of plane No. 2. Similarly, when it continues its descent to plane No. 3, it must draw round itself the matter of that plane, and we shall then have, say, an atom whose body or outer covering consists of the matter of plane No. 3. The force energizing in it – its soul, so to speak – will however not be spirit in the condition in which it was on plane No. 1, but will be that divine force *plus* the veil of the matter of plane No. 2. When a still further descent is made to plane No. 4, the atom becomes still more complex, for it will then have a body of No. 4 matter, ensouled by spirit already twice veiled – in the matter of planes 2 and 3. It will be seen that, since this process repeats itself for every sub-plane of each plane of the solar system, by the time the original force reaches our physical level it is so thoroughly veiled that it is small wonder men often fail to recognize it as spirit at all.

Suppose that the monadic essence has carried on this process of veiling itself down to the atomic level of the mental plane, and that, instead of descending through the various subdivisions of that plane, it plunges down directly into the astral plane, ensouling, or aggregating round it a body of atomic astral matter; such a combination would be the elemental essence of the astral plane, belonging to the third of the great elemental kingdoms – that immediately preceding the mineral. In the course of its 2,401 differentiations on the astral plane it draws to itself many and various combinations of the matter of its several sub-divisions; but these are only temporary, and it still remains essentially one kingdom, whose characteristic is monadic essence involved down to the atomic level of the mental plane only, but manifesting through the atomic matter of the astral plane.

The two higher elemental kingdoms exist and function respectively upon the higher and the lower levels of the mental plane; but we are not at the moment concerned with them.

To speak, as we so often do, of *an* elemental in connection with the group we are now considering is somewhat misleading, for strictly speaking there is no such thing. What we find is a vast store of elemental essence, wonderfully sensitive to the most fleeting human thought, responding with inconceivable delicacy in an infinitesimal fraction of a second to a vibration set up in it even by an entirely unconscious exercise of human will or desire.

But the moment that by the influence of such thought or exercise of will it is molded into a living force – into something that may correctly be described as *an* elemental – it at once ceases to belong to the category we are discussing, and becomes a member of the artificial class. Even then its separate existence is usually of the most evanescent character, and as soon as its impulse has worked itself out it sinks back into the undifferentiated mass of that particular subdivision of elemental essence from which it came.

It would be tedious to attempt to catalogue these subdivisions, and indeed even if a list of them were made it would be unintelligible except to the practical student who can call them up before him and compare them. Some idea of the leading lines of classification can, however, be grasped without much trouble, and may prove of interest.

First comes the broad division which has given the elementals their name – the classification according to the kind of matter which they inhabit. Here, as usual, the septenary character of our evolution shows itself, for there are seven such chief groups, related respectively to the seven states of physical matter – to "earth, water, air, and fire," or to translate from medieval symbolism to modern accuracy of expression, to the solid, the liquid, the gaseous, and the four etheric conditions.

It has long been the custom to pity and despise the ignorance of the alchemists of the middle ages, because they gave the title of "elements" to substances which modern chemistry has discovered to be compounds; but in speaking of them thus slightingly we have done them great injustice, for their knowledge on this subject was really wider, not narrower, than ours. They may or may not have catalogued all the eighty or ninety substances which we now call elements; but they certainly did not apply that name to them, for their occult studies had taught them that in that sense of the word there was but *one* element, of which these and all other forms of matter were but modifications – a truth which some of the greatest chemists of the present day are just beginning to suspect.

The fact is that in this particular case our despised forefathers' analysis went several steps deeper than our own. They understood and were able to observe the ether, which modern science can only postulate as a necessity for its theories; they were aware that it consists of physical matter in four entirely distinct states above the gaseous – a fact which has not yet been re-discovered. They knew that all physical objects consist of matter in one or other of these seven states, and that into the composition of every organic body all seven enter in a greater or lesser degree; hence all their talk of fiery and watery humors, or "elements," which seems so grotesque to us. It is obvious that they used the latter word as a synonym for "constituent parts," without in the least degree intending it to connote the idea of substances which could not be further reduced. They knew also that each of these orders of matter serves as a basis of manifestation for a great class of evolving monadic essence, and so they christened the essence "elemental."

What we have to try to realize, then, is that in every particle of solid matter, so long as it remains in that condition, there resides, to use the picturesque phraseology of medieval students, an earth elemental – that is, a certain amount of the living elemental essence appropriate to it, while equally in every particle of matter in the liquid, gaseous, or etheric states, the water, air, and fire "elementals" respectively in here. It will be observed that this first broad division of the third of the elemental kingdoms is, so to speak, horizontal – that is to say, its respective classes stand in the relation of steps, each somewhat less material than that below it, which ascends into it by almost imperceptible degrees; and it is easy to understand how each of these classes may again he divided horizontally into seven, since there are obviously many degrees of density among solids, liquids, and gases.

There is, however, what may be described as a perpendicular division also, and this is somewhat more difficult to comprehend, especially as great reserve is always maintained by occultists as to some of the facts which would be involved in a fuller explanation of it. Perhaps the clearest way to put what is known on the subject will be to state that in each of the horizontal classes and subclasses will be found seven perfectly distinct types of elemental, the difference between them being no longer a question of degree of materiality, but rather of character and affinities.

Each of these types so reacts upon the others that, though it is impossible for them ever to interchange their essence, in each of them seven sub-types will be found to exist, distinguished by the coloring given to their original peculiarity by the influence which sways them most readily. It will be seen that this perpendicular division and subdivision differs entirely in its character from the horizontal, in that it is far more permanent and fundamental; for while it is the evolution of the elemental kingdom to pass with almost infinite slowness through its various horizontal classes and sub-classes in succession, and thus to belong to them all in turn, this is not so with regard to the types and sub-types, which remain unchangeable all the way through.

A point of which we must never lose sight in endeavoring to understand this elemental evolution is that it is taking place on what is sometimes called the downward curve of the arc; that is to say, it is progressing *towards* the complete entanglement in matter which we witness in the mineral kingdom, instead of *away* from it, as is most other evolution of which we know anything. Thus, for it progress means descent into matter instead of ascent towards higher planes; and this fact sometimes gives it a curiously inverted appearance in our eyes until we thoroughly grasp its object. Unless the student bears this constantly and clearly in mind, he will again and again find himself beset by perplexing anomalies.

In spite of these manifold subdivisions, there are certain properties which are possessed in common by all varieties of this strange living essence; but even these are so entirely different from any with which we are familiar on the physical plane that it is exceedingly difficult to explain them to those who cannot themselves see them in action.

Let it be premised, then, that when any portion of this essence remains for a few moments entirely unaffected by any outside influence (a condition, by the way, which is hardly ever realized) it is absolutely without any definite form of its own, though its motion is still rapid and ceaseless; but on the slightest disturbance, set up perhaps by some passing thought-current, it flashes into a bewildering confusion of restless, ever-changing shapes, which form, rush about, and disappear with the rapidity of the bubbles on the surface of boiling water.

These evanescent shapes, though generally those of living creatures of some sort, human or otherwise, no more express the existence of separate entities in the essence than do the equally changeful and multiform waves raised in a few moments on a previously smooth lake by a sudden squall. They seem to be mere reflections from the vast storehouse of the astral plane, yet they have usually a certain appropriateness to the character of the thought-stream which calls them into existence, though nearly always with some grotesque distortion, some terrifying or unpleasant aspect about them.

A question naturally arises in the mind here as to what intelligence it is that is exerted in the selection of an appropriate shape or its distortion when selected. We are not dealing with the more powerful and longer-lived artificial elemental created by a strong definite thought, but with the result produced by the stream of half-conscious, involuntary thoughts which the majority of mankind allow to flow idly through their brains. The intelligence, therefore, is obviously not derived from the mind of the thinker; and we certainly cannot credit the elemental essence itself, which belongs to a kingdom further from individualization even than the mineral, with any sort of awakening of the mental quality.

Yet it does possess a marvelous adaptability which often seems to come near it, and it is no doubt this property that caused elementals to be described in one of our early books as "the semi-intelligent creatures of the astral light." We shall find further evidence of this power when we come to consider the case of the artificial class. When we read of a good or evil elemental, it must always be either an artificial entity or one of the many varieties of nature-spirits that is meant, for the elemental kingdoms proper do not admit of any such conceptions as good and evil.

There is, however, undoubtedly a sort of bias or tendency permeating nearly all their subdivisions which operates to render them rather hostile than friendly towards man. Every neophyte knows this, for in most cases his very first impression of the astral plane is of the presence all around him of vast hosts of protean specters who advance upon him in threatening guise, but always retire or dissipate harmlessly if boldly faced. It is to this curious tendency that the distorted or unpleasant aspect above mentioned must be referred, and medieval writers tell us that man has only himself to thank for its existence. In the golden age before this sordid present, men were on the whole less selfish and more spiritual, and then the "elementals" were friendly, though now they are so no longer because of man's indifference to, and want of sympathy with, other living beings.

From the wonderful delicacy with which the essence

responds to the faintest action of our minds or desires, it seems clear that this elemental kingdom as a whole is much what the collective thought of humanity makes it. Anyone who will think for a moment how far from elevating the action of that collective thought is likely to be at the present time, will see little reason to wonder that we reap as we have sown, and that this essence, which has no power of perception, but only blindly receives and reflects what is projected upon it, should usually exhibit unfriendly characteristics.

There can be no doubt that in later races or rounds, when mankind as a whole has evolved to a much higher level, the elemental kingdoms will be influenced by the changed thought which continually impinges upon them, and we shall find them no longer hostile, but docile and helpful as we are told that the animal kingdom will also be. Whatever may have happened in the past, it is evident that we may look forward to a passable "golden age" in the future, if we can arrive at a time when the majority of men will be noble and unselfish, and the forces of nature will co-operate willingly with them.

The fact that we are so readily able to influence the elemental kingdoms shows us that we have a responsibility towards them for the manner in which we use that influence. Indeed, when we consider the conditions under which they exist, it is obvious that the effect produced upon them by the thoughts and desires of all intelligent creatures inhabiting the same world with them must have been calculated upon in the scheme of our system as a factor in their evolution.

In spite of the consistent teaching of all the great religions, the mass of mankind is still utterly regardless of its responsibility on the thought-plane; if a man can flatter himself that his words and deeds have been harmless to others, he believes that he has done all that can be required of him, quite oblivious of the fact that he may for years have been exercising a narrowing and debasing influence on the minds of those about him, and filling surrounding space with the unlovely creations of a sordid mind. A still more serious aspect of this question will come before us when we discuss the artificial elemental; but in regard to the essence it will be sufficient to state that we undoubtedly have the power to accelerate or delay its evolution according to the use which, consciously or unconsciously, we are continually making of it.

It would be hopeless within the limits of such a treatise as this to attempt to explain the different uses to which the forces inherent in the manifold varieties of this elemental essence can he put by one who has been trained in their management. The majority of magical ceremonies depend almost entirely upon its manipulation, either directly by the will of the magician, or by some more definite astral entity evoked by him for that purpose.

By its means nearly all the physical phenomena of the *séance*-room are produced, and it is also the agent in most cases of stone-throwing or bell-ringing in haunted houses, such results as these latter being brought about either by blundering efforts to attract attention made by some earth-bound human entity, or by the mere mischievous pranks of some of the minor nature-spirits belonging to our third class. But we must never think of the "elemental" as itself a prime mover; it is simply a latent force, which needs an external power to set it in motion.

Although all classes of the essence have the power of reflecting astral images as described above, there are varieties which receive certain impressions much more readily than others – which have, as it were, favorite forms of their own into which upon disturbance they would naturally flow unless absolutely forced into some other, and such shapes tend to be a trifle less evanescent than usual.

Before leaving this branch of the subject it may be well to warn the student against the confusion of thought into which some have fallen through failing to distinguish this elemental essence which we have been considering from the monadic essence manifesting through the mineral kingdom. Monadic essence at one stage of its evolution towards humanity manifests through the elemental kingdom, while at a later stage it manifests through the mineral kingdom; but the fact that two bodies of monadic essence at these different stages are in manifestation at the same moment, and that one of these manifestations (the earth elemental) occupies the same space as and inhabits the other (say a rock), in no way interferes with the evolution either of one or the other, nor does it imply any relation between the bodies of monadic essence lying within both.

2. *The Astral Bodies of Animals.* This is an extremely large class, yet it does not occupy a particularly important position on the astral plane, since its members usually stay there but a short time. The vast majority of animals have not as yet acquired permanent individualization, and when one of them dies the monadic essence which has been manifesting through it flows back again into the particular stratum whence it came, bearing with it such advancement or experience as has been attained during that life. It is not, however, able to do this quite immediately; the astral body of the animal rearranges itself just as in man's case, and the animal has a real existence on the astral plane, the length of which, though never great, varies according to the intelligence which it has developed. In most cases it does not seem to be more than dreamily conscious, but appears perfectly happy.

The comparatively few domestic animals who have already attained individuality, and will therefore be reborn no more as animals in this world, have a much longer and much more vivid life on the astral plane than their less advanced fellows, and at the end of it sink gradually into a subjective condition, which is likely to last for a very considerable period. One interesting subdivision of this class consists of the astral bodies of those anthropoid apes mentioned in *The Secret Doctrine* who are already individualized, and will be ready to take human incarnation in the next round, or perhaps some of them even sooner.

3. *Nature-Spirits of all Kinds.* So many and so varied are the subdivisions of this class that to do them anything like justice one would need to devote a separate treatise to this subject alone. Some characteristics, however, they all have in common, and it will be sufficient here to try to give some idea of those.

First, we have to realize that we are here dealing with entities which differ radically from all that we have hitherto considered. Though we may rightly classify the elemental essence and the animal astral bodies as non-human, the monadic essence which ensouls them will, nevertheless, in the fullness of time, evolve to the level of manifesting itself through some future humanity comparable to our own, and if we were able to look back through countless ages on our own evolution in previous world-cycles, we should find that that which is now our casual body has passed on its upward path through similar stages.

That, however, is not the case with the vast kingdom of nature-spirits; they neither have been, nor ever will be, members of a humanity such as ours; their line of evolution is entirely different, and their only connection with us consists in our temporary occupancy of the same planet. Of course, since we are neighbors for the time being we owe neighborly kindness to one another when we happen to meet, but our lines of development differ so widely that each can do but little for the other.

Many writers have included these spirits among the elementals, and indeed they are the elementals (or perhaps, to speak more accurately, the animals) of a higher evolution. Though much more highly developed than our elemental essence, they have yet certain characteristics in common with it; for example, they also are divided into seven great classes, inhabiting respectively the same seven states of matter already mentioned as permeated by the corresponding varieties of the essence. Thus, to take those which are most readily comprehensible to us, there are spirits of the earth, water, air, and fire (or ether) – definite intelligent astral entities residing and functioning in each of those media.

It may be asked how it is possible for any kind of creature to inhabit the solid substance of a rock, or of the crust of the earth. The answer is that since the nature-spirits are formed of astral matter, the substance of the rock is no hindrance to their motion or their vision, and furthermore physical matter in its solid state is their natural element – that to which they are accustomed and in which they feel at home. The same is true of those who live in water, air, or ether.

In medieval literature, these earth-spirits are often called gnomes, while the water-spirits are spoken of as undines, the air-spirits as sylphs, and the fire-spirits as salamanders. In popular language they are known by many names – fairies, pixies, elves, brownies, peris, djinns, trolls, satyrs, fauns, kobolds, imps, goblins, good people, etc. – some of these titles being applied only to one variety, and others indiscriminately to all.

Their forms are many and various, but most frequently human in shape and somewhat diminutive in size. Like almost all inhabitants of the astral plane, they are able to assume any appearance at will, but they undoubtedly have definite forms of their own, or perhaps we should rather say favorite forms, which they wear when they have no special object in taking another. Under ordinary conditions they are not visible to physical sight at all, but they have the power of making themselves so by materialization when they wish to be seen.

There are an immense number of subdivisions or races among them, and individuals differ in intelligence and disposition precisely as human beings do. The great majority of them apparently prefer to avoid man altogether; his habits and emanations are distasteful to them, and the constant rush of astral currents set up by his restless, ill-regulated desires disturbs and annoys them. On the other hand, instances are not wanting in which nature spirits have as it were made friends with human beings and offered them such assistance as lay in their power, as in the well-known stories told of the Scotch brownies or of the fire-lighting fairies mentioned in spiritualistic literature.

This helpful attitude, however, is comparatively rare, and in most cases when they come in contact with man, they either show indifference or dislike, or else take an impish delight in deceiving him and playing childish tricks upon him. Many a story illustrative of this curious characteristic may be found among the village gossip of the peasantry in almost any lonely mountainous district; and anyone who has been in the habit of attending *séances* for physical phenomena will recollect instances of practical joking and silly though usually good-natured horse-play, which almost always indicate the presence of some of the lower orders of the nature-spirits.

They are greatly assisted in their tricks by the wonderful power which they possess of casting a glamour over those who yield themselves to their influence, so that such victims for the time see and hear only what these fairies impress upon them, exactly as the mesmerized subject sees, hears, feels, and believes whatever the magnetizer wishes. The nature-spirits, however, have not the mesmerizer's power of dominating the human will, except in the case of quite unusually weak-minded people, or of those who allow themselves to fall into such a condition of helpless terror that their will is temporarily in abeyance. They cannot go beyond deception of the senses, but of that art they are undoubted masters, and cases are not wanting in which they have cast their glamour over a considerable number of people at once. It is by invoking their aid in the exercise of this peculiar power that some of the most wonderful feats of the Indian jugglers are performed – the entire audience being in fact hallucinated and made to imagine that they see and hear a whole series of events which have not really taken place at all.

We might almost look upon the nature-spirits as a kind of astral humanity, but for the fact that none of them – not even the highest – possesses a permanent reincarnating individuality. Apparently, therefore, one point in which their line of evolution differs from ours is that a much greater proportion of intelligence is developed before permanent individualization takes place; but of the stages through which they have passed, and those through which they have yet to pass, we can know little.

The life-periods of the different subdivisions vary greatly, some being quite short, others much longer than our human lifetimes. We stand so entirely outside such a life as theirs that it is impossible for us to understand much about its conditions; but it appears on the whole to be a simple, joyous, irresponsible kind of existence, such as a party of happy children might lead among exceptionally favorable physical surroundings.

Though tricky and mischievous, they are rarely malicious unless provoked by some unwarrantable intrusion or annoyance; but as a body they also partake to some extent of the universal feeling of distrust for man, and they generally seem inclined to resent somewhat the first appearance of a neophyte on the astral plane, so that he usually makes their acquaintance under some unpleasant or terrifying form. If, however, he declines to be frightened by any of their freaks, they soon accept him as a necessary evil and take no further notice of him, while some among them may even after a time become friendly and manifest pleasure on meeting him.

Some among the many subdivisions of this class are much less childlike and more dignified than those we have been describing, and it is from these sections that the lower types among the entities who have been reverenced under the name of wood-gods, or local village-gods, have been drawn. Such entities would be quite sensible of the flattery involved in the reverence shown to them, enjoy it, and are usually quite ready to do any small service they can in return. (The village-god is also often an artificial entity, but that variety will be considered in its appropriate place).

The Adept knows how to make use of the services of the nature-spirits when he requires them, but the ordinary magician can obtain their assistance only by processes either of invocation or evocation – that is, either by attracting their attention as a suppliant and making some kind of bargain with them, or by endeavoring to set in motion influences which would compel their obedience. Both methods are extremely undesirable, and the latter is also excessively dangerous, as the operator arouses a determined hostility which may easily prove fatal to him. Needless to say, no one studying occultism under a qualified Master would ever be permitted to attempt anything of the kind at all.

4. *The Devas.* The highest system of evolution connected with this earth, so far as we know, is that of the beings whom Hindus call the Devas, who are elsewhere described as Angels, sons of God, etc. They may, in fact, be regarded as a kingdom, lying next above humanity, in the same way as humanity in turn lies next above the animal kingdom, but with this important difference, that while for an animal there is no possibility of evolution (so far as we know) through any kingdom but the human man, when he attains a certain high level, finds various paths of advancement opening before him of which this great Deva evolution is only one.

In comparison with the sublime renunciation of the Nirmanakaya, the acceptance of this line of evolution is sometimes mentioned in the books as "yielding to the temptation to become a god", but it must not be inferred from this expression that any shadow of blame attaches to the man who makes this choice. The path which he selects is not the shortest, but it is nevertheless very noble, and if his developed intuition impels him towards it, it is certainly that which is best suited for his capacities. We must never forget that in spiritual as in physical climbing it is not every one who can bear the strain of the steeper path; there may be many for whom what seems the slower way is the only possibility, and we should indeed be unworthy followers of the great Teachers if we allowed our ignorance to betray us into the slightest thought of disposal towards those whose choice differs from our own.

However confident ignorance of the difficulties of the future may allow us to feel now, it is impossible for us to tell at this stage what we shall find ourselves able to do when, after many lives of patient striving, we have earned the right to choose our own future; and indeed, even those who "yield to the temptation to become gods" have a sufficiently glorious career before them, as will presently be seen. To avoid possible misunderstanding it may be that there is another and entirely evil sense sometimes attached in the books to this phrase of "becoming a god," but in that form it certainly could never be any kind of "temptation" to the developed man, and in any case it is altogether foreign to our present subject.

In oriental literature this word "Deva" is frequently used vaguely to mean almost any kind of non-human entity, so that it often includes great divinities on the one hand, and nature-spirits and artificial elementals on the other. Here, however, its use will be restricted to the magnificent evolution which we are now considering.

Though connected with this earth, the Angels are by no means confined to it, for the whole of our present chain of seven worlds is as one world to them, their evolution being through a grand system of seven chains. Their hosts have hitherto been recruited chiefly from other humanities in the solar system, some lower and some higher than ours, since but a very small portion of our own has as yet reached the level at which for us it is possible to join them; but it seems certain that some of their very numerous classes have not passed in their upward progress through any humanity at all comparable to ours.

It is not possible for us at present to understand much about them, but it is clear that what may be described as the aim of their evolution is considerably higher than ours; that is to say, while the object of our human evolution is to raise the successful portion of humanity to a certain degree of occult development by the end of the seventh round, the object of the angelic evolution is to bring their foremost rank to a much higher level in the corresponding period. For them, as for us, a steeper but shorter path to still more sublime heights lies open to earnest endeavor; but what those heights may be in their case we can only conjecture.

It is these Angles who constantly watch all through life to counterbalance the changes perpetually being introduced into man's condition by his own free will and that of those around him, so that no injustice may be done, and karma may be accurately worked out, if not in one way then in another. A learned dissertation upon these marvelous beings will be found in *The Secret Doctrine*. They are able to take human material forms at will, and several cases are recorded when they have done so.

All the higher nature-spirits and hosts of artificial elementals act as their agents in the stupendous work they carry out, yet all the threads are in their hands, and the whole responsibility rests upon them alone. It is not often that they manifest upon the astral plane, but when they do, they are certainly the most remarkable of its non-human inhabitants. A student of occultism will not need to be told that as there are seven great classes both of nature-spirits and elemental essence there must really be seven and not four Devarajas, but outside the circle of Initiation little is known and less may be said.

The Kith of the Elf Folk

by Lord Dunsany

Chapter I

The north wind was blowing, and red and golden the last days of Autumn were streaming hence. Solemn and cold over the marshes arose the evening.

It became very still.

Then the last pigeon went home to the trees on the dry land in the distance, whose shapes already had taken upon themselves a mystery in the haze.

Then all was still again.

As the light faded and the haze deepened, mystery crept nearer from every side.

Then the green plover came in crying, and all alighted.

And again it became still, save when one of the plover rose and flew a little way uttering the cry of the waste. And hushed and silent became the earth, expecting the first star. Then the duck came in, and the widgeon, company by company: and all the light of day faded out of the sky saving one red band of light. Across the light appeared, black and huge, the wings of a flock of geese beating up wind to the marshes. These too went down among the rushes.

Then the stars appeared and shone in the stillness, and there was silence in the great spaces of the night.

Suddenly the bells of the cathedral in the marshes broke out, calling to evensong.

Eight centuries ago on the edge of the marsh men had built the huge cathedral, or it may have been seven centuries ago, or perhaps nine--it was all one to the Wild Things.

So evensong was held, and candles lighted, and the lights through the windows shone red and green in the water, and the sound of the organ, went roaring over the marshes. But from the deep and perilous places, edged with bright mosses, the Wild Things came leaping up to dance on the reflection of the stars, and over their heads as they danced the marsh-lights rose and fell.

The Wild Things are somewhat human in appearance, only all brown of skin and barely two feet high. Their ears are pointed like the squirrel's, only far larger, and they leap to prodigious heights. They live all day under deep pools in the loneliest marshes, but at night they come up and dance. Each Wild Thing has over its head a marsh-light, which moves as the Wild Thing moves; they have no souls, and cannot die, and are of the kith of the Elf-folk.

All night they dance over the marshes, treading upon the reflection of the stars (for the bare surface of the water will not hold them by itself); but when the stars begin to pale, they sink down one by one into the pools of their home. Or if they tarry longer, sitting upon the rushes, their bodies fade from view as the marsh-fires pale in the light, and by daylight none may see the Wild Things of the kith of the Elf-folk. Neither may any see them even at night unless they were born, as I was, in the hour of dusk, just at the moment when the first star appears.

Now, on the night that I tell of, a little Wild Thing had gone drifting over the waste, till it came right up to the walls of the cathedral and danced upon the images of the colored saints as they lay in the water among the reflection of the stars. And as it leaped in its fantastic dance, it saw through the painted windows to where the people prayed, and heard the organ roaring over the marshes. The sound of the organ roared over the marshes, but the song and prayers of the people streamed up from the cathedral's highest tower like thin gold chains, and reached to Paradise, and up and down them went the angels from Paradise to the people, and from the people to Paradise again.

Then something akin to discontent troubled the Wild Thing

for the first time since the making of the marshes; and the soft grey ooze and the chill of the deep water seemed to be not enough, nor the first arrival from northwards of the tumultuous geese, nor the wild rejoicing of the wings of the wildfowl when every feather sings, nor the wonder of the calm ice that comes when the snipe depart and beards the rushes with frost and clothes the hushed waste with a mysterious haze where the sun goes red and low, nor even the dance of the Wild Things in the marvelous night; and the little Wild Thing longed to have a soul, and to go and worship God.

And when evensong was over and the lights were out, it went back crying to its kith.

But on the next night, as soon as the images of the stars appeared in the water, it went leaping away from star to star to the farthest edge of the marshlands, where a great wood grew where dwelt the Oldest of the Wild Things.

And it found the Oldest of Wild Things sitting under a tree, sheltering itself from the moon.

And the little Wild Thing said: "I want to have a soul to worship God, and to know the meaning of music, and to see the inner beauty of the marshlands and to imagine Paradise."

And the Oldest of the Wild Things said to it: "What have we to do with God? We are only Wild Things, and of the kith of the Elf-folk."

But it only answered, "I want to have a soul."

Then the Oldest of the Wild Things said: "I have no soul to give you; but if you got a soul, one day you would have to die, and if you knew the meaning of music you would learn the meaning of sorrow, and it is better to be a Wild Thing and not to die."

So it went weeping away.

But they that were kin to the Elf-folk were sorry for the little Wild Thing; and though the Wild Things cannot sorrow long, having no souls to sorrow with, yet they felt for awhile a soreness where their souls should be, when they saw the grief of their comrade.

So the kith of the Elf-folk went abroad by night to make a soul for the little Wild Thing. And they went over the marshes till they came to the high fields among the flowers and grasses. And there they gathered a large piece of gossamer that the spider had laid by twilight; and the dew was on it.

Into this dew had shone all the lights of the long banks of the ribbed sky, as all the colors changed in the restful spaces of evening. And over it the marvelous night had gleamed with all its stars.

Then the Wild Things went with their dew-bespangled gossamer down to the edge of their home. And there they gathered a piece of the grey mist that lies by night over the marshlands. And into it they put the melody of the waste that is borne up and down the marshes in the evening on the wings of the golden plover. And they put into it too the mournful song that the reeds are compelled to sing before the presence of the arrogant North Wind. Then each of the Wild Things gave some treasured memory of the old marshes, "For we can spare it," they said. And to all this they added a few images of the stars that they gathered out of the water. Still the soul that the kith of the Elf-folk were making had no life.

Then they put into it the low voices of two lovers that went walking in the night, wandering late alone. And after that they waited for the dawn. And the queenly dawn appeared, and the marsh-lights of the Wild Things paled in the glare, and their bodies faded from view; and still they waited by the marsh's edge. And to them waiting came over field and marsh, from the ground and out of the sky, the myriad song of the birds.

This too the Wild Things put into the piece of haze that they had gathered in the marshlands, and wrapped it all up in their dew-bespangled gossamer. Then the soul lived.

And there it lay in the hands of the Wild Things no larger than a hedgehog; and wonderful lights were in it, green and blue; and they changed ceaselessly, going round and round; and in the grey midst of it was a purple flare.

And the next night they came to the little Wild Thing and showed her the gleaming soul. And they said to her: "If you must have a soul and go and worship God, and become a mortal and die, place this to your left breast a little above the heart, and it will enter and you will become a human. But if you take it you can never be rid of it to become immortal again unless you pluck it out and give it to another; and we will not take it, and most of the humans have a soul already. And if you cannot find a human without a soul you will one day die, and your soul cannot go to Paradise, because it was only made in the marshes."

Far away the little Wild Thing saw the cathedral windows alight for evensong, and the song of the people mounting up to Paradise, and all the angels going up and down. So it bid farewell with tears and thanks to the Wild Things of the kith of Elf-folk, and went leaping away towards the green dry land, holding the soul in its hands.

And the Wild Things were sorry that it had gone, but could not be sorry long, because they had no souls.

At the marsh's edge the little Wild Thing gazed for some moments over the water to where the marsh-fires were leaping up and down, and then pressed the soul against its left breast a little above the heart.

Instantly it became a young and beautiful woman, who was cold and frightened. She clad herself somehow with bundles of reeds, and went towards the lights of a house that stood close by. And she pushed open the door and entered, and found a farmer and a farmer's wife sitting over their supper.

And the farmer's wife took the little Wild Thing with the soul of the marshes up to her room, and clothed her and braided her hair, and brought her down again, and gave her the first food that she had ever eaten. Then the farmer's wife asked many questions.

"Where have you come from?" she said.

"Over the marshes."

"From what direction?" said the farmer's wife.

"South," said the little Wild Thing with the new soul.

"But none can come over the marshes from the south," said the farmer's wife.

"No, they can't do that," said the farmer.

"I lived in the marshes."

"Who are you?" asked the farmer's wife.

"I am a Wild Thing, and have found a soul in the marshes, and we are kin to the Elf-folk."

Talking it over afterwards, the farmer and his wife agreed that she must be a gipsy who had been lost, and that she was queer with hunger and exposure.

So that night the little Wild Thing slept in the farmer's house, but her new soul stayed awake the whole night long dreaming of the beauty of the marshes.

As soon as dawn came over the waste and shone on the farmer's house, she looked from the window towards the glittering waters, and saw the inner beauty of the marsh. For the Wild Things only love the marsh and know its haunts, but now she perceived the mystery of its distances and the glamour of its perilous pools, with their fair and deadly mosses, and felt the marvel of the North Wind who comes dominant out of unknown icy lands, and the wonder of that ebb and flow of life when the wildfowl whirl in at evening to the marshlands and at dawn pass out to sea. And she knew that over her head above the farmer''s house stretched wide Paradise, where perhaps God was now imagining a sunrise while angels played low on lutes, and the sun came rising up on the world below to gladden fields and marsh.

And all that heaven thought, the marsh thought too; for the blue of the marsh was as the blue of heaven, and the great cloud shapes in heaven became the shapes in the marsh, and through each ran momentary rivers of purple, errant between banks of gold. And the stalwart army of reeds appeared out of the gloom with all their pennons waving as far as the eye could see. And from another window she saw the vast cathedral gathering its ponderous strength together, and lifting it up in towers out of the marshlands.

She said, "I will never, never leave the marsh."

An hour later she dressed with great difficulty and went down to eat the second meal of her life. The farmer and his wife were kindly folk, and taught her how to eat.

"I suppose the gipsies don't have knives and forks," one said to the other afterwards.

After breakfast the farmer went and saw the Dean, who lived near his cathedral, and presently returned and brought back to the Dean's house the little Wild Thing with the new soul.

"This is the lady," said the farmer. "This is Dean Murnith." Then he went away.

"Ah," said the Dean, "I understand you were lost the other night in the marshes. It was a terrible night to be lost in the marshes."

"I love the marshes," said the little Wild Thing with the new soul.

"Indeed! How old are you?" said the Dean.

"I don't know," she answered.

"You must know about how old you are," he said.

"Oh, about ninety," she said, "or more."

"Ninety years!" exclaimed the Dean.

"No, ninety centuries," she said; "I am as old as the marshes."

Then she told her story--how she had longed to be a human and go and worship God, and have a soul and see the beauty of the world, and how all the Wild Things had made her a soul of gossamer and mist and music and strange memories.

"But if this is true," said Dean Murnith, "this is very wrong. God cannot have intended you to have a soul."

"What is your name?"

"I have no name," she answered.

"We must find a Christian name and a surname for you. What would you like to be called?"

"Song of the Rushes," she said.

"That won't do at all," said the Dean.

"Then I would like to be called Terrible North Wind, or Star in the Waters," she said.

"No, no, no," said Dean Murnith; "that is quite impossible. We could call you Miss Rush if you like. How would Mary Rush do? Perhaps you had better have another name--say Mary Jane Rush."

So the little Wild Thing with the soul of the marshes took the names that were offered her, and became Mary Jane Rush.

"And we must find something for you to do," said Dean Murnith. "Meanwhile we can give you a room here."

"I don't want to do anything," replied Mary Jane; "I want to worship God in the cathedral and live beside the marshes."

Then Mrs. Murnith came in, and for the rest of that day Mary Jane stayed at the house of the Dean.

And there with her new soul she perceived the beauty of the world; for it came grey and level out of misty distances, and widened into grassy fields and plough lands right up to the edge of an old gabled town; and solitary in the fields far off an ancient windmill stood, and his honest handmade sails went round and round in the free East Anglian winds. Close by, the gabled houses leaned out over the streets, planted fair upon sturdy timbers that grew in the olden time, all glorying among themselves upon their beauty. And out of them, buttress by buttress, growing and going upwards, aspiring tower by tower, rose the cathedral.

And she saw the people moving in the streets all leisurely and slow, and unseen among them, whispering to each other, unheard by living men and concerned only with bygone things, drifted the ghosts of very long ago. And wherever the streets ran eastwards, wherever were gaps in the houses, always there broke into view the sight of the great marshes, like to some bar of music weird and strange that haunts a melody, arising again and again, played on the violin by one musician only, who plays no other bar, and he is swart and lank about the hair and bearded about the lips, and his moustache droops long and low, and no one knows the land from which he comes.

All these were good things for a new soul to see.

Then the sun set over green fields and ploughland, and the night came up. One by one the merry lights of cheery lamp-lit windows took their stations in the solemn night.

Then the bells rang, far up in a cathedral tower, and their melody fell on the roofs of the old houses and poured over their eaves until the streets were full, and then flooded away over green fields and plough, till it came to the sturdy mill and brought the miller trudging to evensong, and far away eastwards and seawards the sound rang out over the remoter marshes. And it was all as yesterday to the old ghosts in the streets.

Then the Dean's wife took Mary Jane to evening service, and she saw three hundred candles filling all the aisle with light. But sturdy pillars stood there in unlit vastnesses; great colonnades going away into the gloom, where evening and morning, year in year out, they did their work in the dark, holding the cathedral roof aloft. And it was stiller than the marshes are still when the ice has come and the wind that brought it has fallen.

Suddenly into this stillness rushed the sound of the organ, roaring, and presently the people prayed and sang.

No longer could Mary Jane see their prayers ascending like thin gold chains, for that was but an elfin fancy, but she imagined clear in her new soul the seraphs passing in the ways of Paradise, and the angels changing guard to watch the World by night.

When the Dean had finished service, a young curate, Mr. Millings, went up into the pulpit.

He spoke of Abana and Pharpar, rivers of Damascus: and Mary Jane was glad that there were rivers having such names, and heard with wonder of Nineveh, that great city, and many things strange and new.

And the light of the candles shone on the curate's fair hair, and his voice went ringing down the aisle, and Mary Jane rejoiced that he was there.

But when his voice stopped she felt a sudden loneliness, such as she had not felt since the making of the marshes; for the Wild Things never are lonely and never unhappy, but dance all night on the reflection of the stars, and, having no souls, desire nothing more.

After the collection was made, before anyone moved to go, Mary Jane walked up the aisle to Mr. Millings.

"I love you," she said.

Chapter II

Nobody sympathized with Mary Jane. "So unfortunate for Mr. Millings," every one said; "such a promising young man."

Mary Jane was sent away to a great manufacturing city of the Midlands, where work had been found for her in a cloth factory, And there was nothing in that town that was good for a soul to see. For it did not know that beauty was to be desired; so it made many things by machinery, and became hurried in all its ways, and boasted its superiority over other cities and became richer and richer, and there was none to pity it.

In this city Mary Jane had had lodgings found for her near the factory.

At six o'clock on those November mornings, about the time that, far away from the city, the wildfowl rose up out of the calm marshes and passed to the troubled spaces of the sea, at six o'clock the factory uttered a prolonged howl and gathered the workers together, and there they worked, saving two hours for food, the whole of the daylit hours and into the dark till the bells tolled six again.

There Mary Jane worked with other girls in a long dreary room, where giants sat pounding wool into a long thread-like strip with iron, rasping hands. And all day long they roared as they sat at their soulless work. But the work of Mary Jane was not with these, only their roar was ever in her ears as their clattering iron limbs went to and fro.

Her work was to tend a creature smaller, but infinitely more cunning.

It took the strip of wool that the giants had threshed, and whirled it round and round until it had twisted it into hard thin thread. Then it would make a clutch with fingers of steel at the thread that it had gathered, and waddle away about five yards and come back with more.

It had mastered all the subtlety of skilled workers, and had gradually displaced them; one thing only it could not do, it was unable to pick up the ends if a piece of the thread broke, in order to tie them together again. For this a human soul was required, and it was Mary Jane's business to pick up broken ends; and the moment she placed them together the busy soulless creature tied them for itself.

All here was ugly; even the green wool as it whirled round and round was neither the green of the grass nor yet the green of the rushes, but a sorry muddy green that befitted a sullen city under a murky sky.

When she looked out over the roofs of the town, there too was ugliness; and well the houses knew it, for with hideous stucco they aped in grotesque mimicry the pillars and temples of old Greece, pretending to one another to be that which they were not. And emerging from these houses and going in, and seeing the pretense of paint and stucco year after year until it all peeled away, the souls of the poor owners of those houses sought to be other souls until they grew weary of it.

At evening Mary Jane went back to her lodgings. Only then, after the dark had fallen, could the soul of Mary Jane perceive any beauty in that city, when the lamps were lit and here and there a star shone through the smoke. Then she would have gone abroad and beheld the night, but this the old woman to whom she was confided would not let her do. And the days multiplied themselves by seven and became weeks, and the weeks passed by, and all days were the same. And all the while the soul of Mary Jane was crying for beautiful things, and found not one, saving on Sundays, when she went to church, and left it to find the city greyer than before.

One day she decided that it was better to be a wild thing in the lovely marshes, than to have a soul that cried for beautiful things and found not one. From that day she determined to be rid of her soul, so she told her story to one of the factory girls, and said to her:

"The other girls are poorly clad and they do soulless work; surely some of them have no souls and would take mine."

200

But the factory girl said to her: "All the poor have souls. It is all they have."

Then Mary Jane watched the rich whenever she saw them, and vainly sought for some one without a soul.

One day at the hour when the machines rested and the human beings that tended them rested too, the wind being at that time from the direction of the marshlands, the soul of Mary Jane lamented bitterly. Then, as she stood outside the factory gates, the soul irresistibly compelled her to sing, and a wild song came from her lips, hymning the marshlands. And into her song came crying her yearning for home, and for the sound of the shout of the North Wind, masterful and proud, with his lovely lady the Snow; and she sang of tales that the rushes murmured to one another, tales that the teal knew and the watchful heron. And over the crowded streets her song went crying away, the song of waste places and of wild free lands, full of wonder and magic, for she had in her elf-made soul the song of the birds and the roar of the organ in the marshes.

At this moment Signor Thompsoni, the well-known English tenor, happened to go by with a friend. They stopped and listened; everyone stopped and listened.

"There has been nothing like this in Europe in my time," said Signor Thompsoni.

So a change came into the life of Mary Jane.

People were written to, and finally it was arranged that she should take a leading part in the Covent Garden Opera in a few weeks.

So she went to London to learn.

London and singing lessons were better than the City of the Midlands and those terrible machines. Yet still Mary Jane was not free to go and live as she liked by the edge of the marshlands, and she was still determined to be rid of her soul, but could find no one that had not a soul of their own.

One day she was told that the English people would not

listen to her as Miss Rush, and was asked what more suitable name she would like to be called by.

"I would like to be called Terrible North Wind," said Mary Jane, "or Song of the Rushes."

When she was told that this was impossible and Signorina Maria Russiano was suggested, she acquiesced at once, as she had acquiesced when they took her away from her curate; she knew nothing of the ways of humans.

At last the day of the Opera came round, and it was a cold day of the winter.

And Signorina Russiano appeared on the stage before a crowded house.

And Signorina Russiano sang.

And into the song went all the longing of her soul, the soul that could not go to Paradise, but could only worship God and know the meaning of music, and the longing pervaded that Italian song as the infinite mystery of the hills is borne along the sound of distant sheep-bells. Then in the souls that were in that crowded house arose little memories of a great while since that were quite dead, and lived awhile again during that marvelous song.

And a strange chill went into the blood of all that listened, as though they stood on the border of bleak marshes and the North Wind blew.

And some it moved to sorrow and some to regret, and some to an unearthly joy--then suddenly the song went wailing away, like the winds of the winter from the marshlands when Spring appears from the South.

So it ended. And a great silence fell fog-like over all that house, breaking in upon the end of a chatty conversation that Cecilia, Countess of Birmingham was enjoying with a friend.

In the dead hush Signorina Russiano rushed from the stage; she appeared again running among the audience, and dashed up to

Lady Birmingham.

"Take my soul," she said; "it is a beautiful soul. It can worship God, and knows the meaning of music and can imagine Paradise. And if you go to the marshlands with it you will see beautiful things; there is an old town there built of lovely timbers, with ghosts in its streets."

Lady Birmingham stared. Everyone was standing up. "See," said Signorina Russiano, "it is a beautiful soul."

And she clutched at her left breast a little above the heart, and there was the soul shining in her hand, with the green and blue lights going round and round and the purple flare in the midst.

"Take it," she said, "and you will love all that is beautiful, and know the four winds, each one by his name, and the songs of the birds at dawn. I do not want it, because I am not free. Put it to your left breast a little above the heart."

Still everybody was standing up, and Lady Birmingham felt uncomfortable.

"Please offer it to some one else," she said.

"But they all have souls already," said Signorina Russiano.

And everybody went on standing up. And Lady Birmingham took the soul in her hand.

"Perhaps it is lucky," she said.

She felt that she wanted to pray.

She half-closed her eyes, and said "*Unberufen*". Then she put the soul to her left breast a little above the heart, and hoped that the people would sit down and the singer go away.

Instantly a heap of clothes collapsed before her. For a moment, in the shadow among the seats, those who were born in the dusk hour might have seen a little brown thing leaping free from the clothes; then it sprang into the bright light of the hall, and became invisible to any human eye.

It dashed about for a little, then found the door, and presently was in the lamplit streets.

To those that were born in the dusk hour it might have been seen leaping rapidly wherever the streets ran northwards and eastwards, disappearing from human sight as it passed under the lamps, and appearing again beyond them with a marsh-light over its head.

Once a dog perceived it and gave chase, and was left far behind.

The cats of London, who are all born in the dusk hour, howled fearfully as it went by.

Presently it came to the meaner streets, where the houses are smaller. Then it went due north-eastwards, leaping from roof to roof. And so in a few minutes it came to more open spaces, and then to the desolate lands, where market gardens grow, which are neither town nor country. Till at last the good black trees came into view, with their demoniac shapes in the night, and the grass was cold and wet, and the night-mist floated over it. And a great white owl came by, going up and down in the dark. And at all these things the little Wild Thing rejoiced elvishly.

And it left London far behind it, reddening the sky, and could distinguish no longer its unlovely roar, but heard again the noises of the night.

And now it would come through a hamlet glowing and comfortable in the night; and now to the dark, wet, open fields again; and many an owl it overtook as they drifted through the night, a people friendly to the Elf-folk. Sometimes it crossed wide rivers, leaping from star to star; and, choosing its way as it went, to avoid the hard, rough roads, came before midnight to the East Anglian lands.

And it heard there the shout of the North Wind, who was dominant and angry, as he drove southwards his adventurous geese; while the rushes bent before him chaunting plaintively and low, like enslaved rowers of some fabulous trireme, bending and swinging under blows of the lash, and singing all the while a doleful song.

And it felt the good dank air that clothes by night the broad East Anglian lands, and came again to some old perilous pool where the soft green mosses grew, and there plunged downward and downward into the dear dark water, till it felt the homely ooze once more coming up between its toes. Thence, out of the lovely chill that is in the heart of the ooze, it arose renewed and rejoicing to dance upon the image of the stars.

I chanced to stand that night by the marsh's edge, forgetting in my mind the affairs of men; and I saw the marsh-fires come leaping up from all the perilous places. And they came up by flocks the whole night long to the number of a great multitude, and danced away together over the marshes.

And I believe that there was a great rejoicing all that night among the kith of the Elf-folk.